CAS
Cassutt, Michael.
The star country

$12.95

The Star Country

The Star Country

MICHAEL CASSUTT

49,622

DOUBLEDAY & COMPANY, INC.

GARDEN CITY, NEW YORK

1986

All of the characters in this book
are fictitious, and any resemblance
to actual persons, living or dead,
is purely coincidental.

Library of Congress Cataloging-in-Publication Data
Cassutt, Michael.
The star country.
I. Title.
PS3553.A812S73   1986   813'.54   86-2106
ISBN: 0-385-19846-9

For Kathryn Kramer Williams
in memory of
Clyde Williams
Leo Francis Cassutt
and
Anastasia Downey Cassutt

The Star Country

CHAPTER 1

People's Republic of Chicago, Sunday Night

Lisa Marquez had just finished unpacking when someone knocked at her door. "It's open!"

Doug Shapiro, one of the mission's second secretaries, put his head in. "Sorry to bother you, Doctor. Did you hear about the latest changes?"

"What changes?" She stuffed the last of her empty bags into the tiny hotel closet. "Hey, you don't have to stand in the hall. Come in."

"Thanks." Shapiro squeezed past, noting the view outside. "Nice. I see Special Assistants rate windows."

The Hilton looked down on an ancient park which lay bare and peaceful under a thin blanket of snow. In the distance, toward the lake, there was an ice rink upon which pairs of stolid, well-bundled Chicagoans glided in the pale sunset. It was so pretty that Lisa hardly noticed the barricades separating the hotel from the park.

"Nice for Chicago, you mean."

"Well, yeah." Shapiro smiled. He was twenty-eight, five years her junior, thin, quiet, and all but invisible until you knew him awhile. They had become friends of a sort in the last two months. "My grandfather got his head busted down there, you know."

"In People's Park? When was this—during the War?" Lisa had turned on the TV, quickly sampling the three official channels serving the People's Republic, to her regret. She left the set on, however; while her own counterbugging devices were in place, a dose of good old white noise never hurt—in the unlikely case anyone happened to be listening in.

"Oh, long before the War. Last century, in fact, about 1970. There was a riot during a political convention, Nixon's or Reagan's, someone like that. Grandpa got arrested and roughed up and thrown in jail, along with a couple of hundred other kids. I guess it was a pretty big deal. He used to *talk* about it like it was."

Lisa stepped up to the window, wishing for a contraband cigarette or, at the very least, an illegal drink.—"So you come by your deviationist tendencies naturally. I have to say I'm shocked to think that a counterrevolutionary like you could reach a position of responsibility in the service of the Great States of Texas." They both laughed at that. "Changes in *what*, Douglas?"

"Oh, sorry: itinerary."

"Really?" She kept a casual expression and tone—she'd had lots of practice—but began to worry. "Getting out of Chicago a day early, something like that?"

"No such luck. There's been what can kindly be described as a hitch in the negotiations with the Californians."

"A major hitch?" She *really* wanted that cigarette now.

"I'd say so. They're canceling the whole L.A. conference."

Damn! "Does anybody know why?"

"No one talks to me, but I get the feeling it had to do with basic admission criteria and access. The Californians want more than the Africans are willing to give."

"Christ, Douglas, *everybody* wants his people to have first crack at the Hocq when they come to town. They were probably just bluffing anyway. The 'workers' paradise' here gave us a lot of trouble, too, but here we are."

"Tell that to Bannekker and his buddies—"

"Those clowns."

"—All I know is, we'll make the stop in Minneapolis as scheduled and then go home. No Denver, no L.A."

"Great." She did not have to fake a tone of annoyance. "Do the Hocq know yet?"

"The Governor was on her way up there a while ago."

"I hope they take this better than they usually take bad news."

"Yeah, it'd be tough to explain to the folks back home that we let the Governor get eaten by aliens from outer space."

Lisa couldn't help smiling. "Still, it's too bad. I was hoping to try surfing."

"You're originally from that area, aren't you?"

"I was born there, yeah."

"Well . . . maybe next year," Shapiro said. "I'd better finish my appointed rounds."

"Thanks for giving me the news."

When she was alone again she had to fight a strong urge to throw some heavy object against the wall. As soon as that impotent anger subsided she allowed herself to get depressed. The whole plan depended on that rendezvous in Denver . . . Could the two of them now escape across fifteen hundred miles of hostile countryside? What a horrible idea.

The phone rang. She knew who it would be.

Lisa was used to his voice by now, an accomplishment she would have thought impossible only a few months ago. Each member of the Hocq mission spoke English, of course—but with the assistance of voders that made them sound like terribly grammatical car crashes. Harrek was one of the more understandable ones, but listening to him still gave her a headache.

"I assume you've heard the news," she said.

"Yes," the alien rasped. "Very distressing."

Aware that they might be under surveillance, Lisa was forced into the ridiculous position of communicating with an extraterrestrial by means of an improvised code. "How are you feeling?" she asked, knowing that, physically, Harrek was fine. "Are your greater knees still giving you trouble?"

"I still suffer," the alien replied.

Lisa could easily picture Harrek, hunched by the telephone in the penthouse several floors overhead, the room crammed with support equipment . . . and three other Hocq, including Big Bad Boroz. "Has the . . . uh, doctor given you any medication?"

"Not yet." There was a pause. "She wishes to continue the treatment."

Oh my God, he wants to go through with it! "Is that even possible?"

"There is no choice."

Was he telling her that one of his sisters suspected? It was probably inevitable that their plan would leak. You couldn't keep a defection a secret forever—

"Maybe I *can* help you out. There's some special medication in cruiser three, down in the garage."

"I'll meet you there," Harrek said.

She took a deep breath and looked around the tacky hotel room. These were probably her final moments as a good citizen of Texas. "Ten minutes," she said.

"That will be satisfactory."

She hung up, wanting only to lie down and sleep, preferably for a week—and that was sure sign that she was terrified. Relax. The worst they can do is kill you! Then she tried to pack her clothes, think about money, worry about her career, wonder about her skill with the cruiser, all at the same time. Another sign of terror. Calm down, kid. One step at a time. Pack up the clothes, the essentials. Forget about money right now: you'll have to make do with what you've got in your purse, since Chicago is closed on a Sunday night and hustling a few hundred bucks from other members of the mission would only raise suspicions. The keys to cruiser three? Ask Shapiro.

Poor Douglas.

She took one last glance out the window. It was completely dark now. The skaters were gone and even the lines seemed shorter in front of the distant shops.

Slinging a single bag over her shoulder, she hurried out.

CHAPTER 2

Central States of America, Monday Morning

"You'd best slow down," Ben Clayton said. "The road's washed out right around this turn."

Jeremy tugged the reins to his left and the wagon rattled noisily, tilting to one side as its wheels slipped off the cracked pavement of the highway and bit into the rutted shoulder. The lone horse tossed her head in protest, but Jeremy urged her along with the leather.

"Ease up on her a bit," Ben told him. "She'll find her way. The town isn't going anywhere."

"Sorry. I've never driven on this kind of road before."

"It's just one of the old state highways—Iowa 56. Used to be as smooth as a baby's behind and it'd take you all the way from the Hill to downtown West Union in no time. That was a few years ago, of course." Ben blinked in the cool early-morning breeze and played with the ornate rings on his fingers. His hands were raw already. "I suppose I should have taken you on this drive before now."

"There are a lot of things we should have done before now," his son replied. "Why pick today to start worrying about it? Besides, you'd still have to come along. I don't know where to go, I don't know who to talk to, and I sure as hell don't know what I'm supposed to say."

Ben grunted. He had been driving down to West Union once every other month for the past fifteen years. He was the official trader for the people of Arrowsmith—as much as anything in the community was ever "official"—having inherited the job from Dan Aucheron, once the old man finally realized that it was time to let someone else

run the risk of contamination in the wicked Outside world. Ben was
a good choice for the job. Born in the community's second generation forty-five years ago—before the changing climate and economic
collapse devasted the Outside and brought on the endless civil wars
—he was loyal enough to be trusted and bright enough to know a
bargain when he saw one.

And over the years he had hauled wagons full of hand-carved
furniture and woolens, fat tomatoes and golden corn, moonshine and
marijuana, whatever the community produced, into town to trade for
items they could not make or scavenge themselves: copper tubing for
the solar heating systems, and for the still; most kinds of medicine;
some tools; plastic containers for food storage; kerosene; wire; material for the storage batteries (though none of that for a long time
now); and rarest of all, news. It was all very well for the people of
Arrowsmith to talk about living in complete harmony with the
planet, using only renewable resources . . . it was quite another
matter to go back to the Stone Age.

But today the wagon was empty.

They'd gone through a long spell of bad luck. Fields that drowned
in last spring's flood brought forth crops only to have them burn in
the unusually hot August sun. The weather was a challenge for the
huge corporate farms in the area. For fields that had endured over
sixty years of haphazard "experimental" farming it was a disaster.
Sickness—measles and flu, especially—paid them a visit with every
change of season, and there had been that horrible bug some years
back that was either cholera or (so they said down at Kelleher's) a
Texan chemical weapon. All of that thinned their numbers, as did
the occasional fires and drownings and accidents—the usual fatal
everyday mishaps. And, in spite of what Dan said or believed, there
was still a trickle of defections to the Outside.

You could go just so far without food, without hope—and there
was little left of either. Their perfect, self-sufficient commune, the
New Age dream of the 1970s—a little world without smog, freeways,
the draft, or middle-class rules—had survived the collapse of the
Outside world by about thirty years.

"Damn." He had spoken out loud, which apparently startled Jeremy, who took his eyes off the road for a second. "Watch out here," Ben said, reaching for the reins. "I told you—"

It was too late. One of the wheels got caught in a rut and began to slide toward the ditch, taking the whole wagon with it. Together Jeremy and Ben managed to head up the horse and keep the wagon from turning on its side, but now they were stuck. Both men climbed down from their seats and pushed, and after a few minutes the wagon pulled free.

"Let me rest a moment," Ben said. He was a sturdy man, but a diet of cornmeal left you with a chalky taste in your mouth, a chronic tightness in your bowels, and very little strength. And then there was that nagging pain deep in his chest.

Jeremy didn't seem too anxious to push on. He squatted against the rear wheel and unbuttoned his bright-colored coat. He was tall for a member of the community and a bit on the thin side. He came by his thinness naturally—his mother, Elizabeth, was still as slim as a cattail. His face had sharp features, notably a prominent nose that he shared with Ben, a broad forehead that made his eyes look deeper than they really were, and brown hair that curled down to his neck. His beard was nicely full, with the exception of a place on his right cheek where he'd been accidentally introduced to Ben's scythe when he was six. Ben still remembered the incident with horror, grateful to this day that he was in the habit of keeping all his tools well cleaned and oiled. Those precautions had probably saved Jeremy from tetanus. Was it then that he allowed himself to take a special interest in the boy? You weren't supposed to, even if you were a biological parent, since all the children of the community deserved equal attention. But Jeremy had been, by far, the brightest and most likable child in Hill House, and once Ben had gotten permanently involved with Elizabeth, the boy's mother, it was impossible to stay away and let others watch him and teach him.

Enough of that. Ben stood up. For autumn, in this land, it was a beautiful morning. Just up, the sun poked through the clouds and steamed the frost off the road. It wasn't uncomfortably cold and, up on a hill like this, heading toward West Union, you could see far up the wooded valley of the Turkey River to the almost endless fields beyond. It was a peaceful sight and it never failed to fill him with a sense of belonging. This was home.

He stretched and said, "Let's get back on the road."

Jeremy was looking at the sky. "I think I hear something."

Before Ben could ask, from far behind them came a whistling that soon grew to a full-throated roar. The poor horse reared and tried to pull the wagon into the ditch again. Ben looked back toward Arrowsmith and saw a dark shape eclipse the sun. Then it screamed over them with a wind that blasted like a tornado.

Suddenly everything was quiet again.

In the distance, down the river valley, a silver bullet sped toward West Union, hugging the curving highway, hopping over the hills as if they were steps in a stairway, until it flew completely out of sight.

"What was *that?*" Jeremy demanded.

"I believe that's what they call a tricar," Ben told him. "It's sort of a motorized wagon that goes on the ground or through the air or on the water. Every now and then somebody down at Kelleher's mentions one." He felt puzzled. "I don't know what it was doing out here."

The boy was bringing the wagon around. He barely stopped long enough for Ben to climb aboard, then slapped the horse into a canter. Ben got ready to chew him out again, then caught sight of the new light in his son's eyes. For the first time in months, it seemed, Jeremy looked interested in being alive. Let him go.

The wagon rattled down the former Iowa 56 at a speed Ben charitably classed as one full notch below breakneck.

CHAPTER 3

West Union, CSA, Monday Morning

The driving got easier the closer they came to West Union. It was all downhill, for one thing, and the highway also began to show signs of recent repair. Dirt roads branching off in both directions bore fresh tracks, and Ben and Jeremy passed half a dozen occupied houses— all of them, to Jeremy's vast disappointment, much smaller than those of Arrowsmith. But he halfway expected that. Even though in his whole life he had never traveled more than a day's walk from Hill House, he knew that West Union wasn't much, as Outside cities went. However, it would do for the moment, especially since the thrill of the tricar encounter had not worn off. He was anxious to see more.

"How many people live here?" he asked.

"A thousand or so," Ben said, "more or less. I got stuck down here on a Saturday night about six years ago, when they had the whole crew in from Martin Farms. You had to fight your way across the street. I think they might have gone as high as *two* thousand in population that night . . . and a lot of them were drunk." He coughed and spat toward the ditch, which was now straight and lined with concrete. "Don't worry, you won't be seeing too many at all this early."

"That's good."

Ben slapped him on the shoulder and laughed. "I thought you *wanted* to come along? See the big city?"

"I did." He was telling the truth—but that was when he had been safe at Hill House and surrounded by a few dozen people at most. "I just don't know what to expect, I guess."

"Oh, they're not all that different, Jeremy, people down here. You know better than to pay attention to what Dan says. Sure, they've got a few toys that we don't bother with and they're hooked into the world information net and they've got a city council that keeps you from parking your wagon in front of the stores, and they've got the Central States Alliance to run Martin Farms and send the troops out any time there's an outlaw scare—but mostly they just breathe and make babies and bitch about the weather. Just like you and me."

"I hope they *eat* like you and me."

"Well, we'll wait and see about that." Ben shifted in his seat and said, "Stop at this corner here, and if there's nothing coming, make a right."

Suddenly they were in West Union. For the next quarter hour Jeremy followed Ben's directions, which was difficult, because he kept swiveling his head around, amazed at the number of buildings. He gradually revised upward his original low estimate of West Union's place in the Outside world. Yet something seemed to be missing. The horse's clacking hoofbeats echoed in the streets. "It seems so empty," he said, finally.

"I told you, it's pretty early for most folks here."

Jeremy didn't know quite what to think of that. They left Hill House at a time when he normally would have been getting up to do the milking (had they any surviving cows) and by now the sun was clearly up in the east, though the shadows here in the valley were still quite long.

Then he saw two figures ahead on the next block. "There's somebody," he said.

"Stop the wagon and be quiet!" Ben hissed. Jeremy did as he was told.

The two blue-clad figures ambled across the street carrying steaming cups from which they drank. Both had rifles slung across their backs. They wore heavy boots, stocking caps, and long coats.

"Just sit still for a minute," Ben said. "Those are CSA soldiers, probably just making routine checks. They won't see us if they don't turn around . . ."

Jeremy's heart drummed in his chest. "What will they do if they see us?"

"Nothing—I think. But you can never tell with some of these people."

The troopers climbed into a tiny, boxlike vehicle, and drove away without a backward glance.

"Okay, now we can go."

They continued on down the street in the same direction as the troopers, past a shabby-looking café which bore a lighted sign identifying it as the Sweet Pea. The customers must not have cared about the grimy exterior. Jeremy counted at least half a dozen at the counter, including one young man who glanced out in time to stare at the passing wagon and its strange occupants.

"We have to pull off the street right up there," Ben said, pointing to a sprawling complex of buildings that was separated from the main street by a flat apron of cracked and pitted asphalt. This was

KELLEHER'S MERCHANDISE MART
Since 1950!
FURNITURE . . . APPLIANCES . . . MARKET

The "R" in "Mart" was only partly there and the barred windows were dark, but there was light enough to show Jeremy that inside the store were indescribable treasures.

"Watch where you're going, boy!" Ben snapped.

Jeremy felt his face redden. "Let's park her right here," Ben said. "Don't worry about tying her up; she won't run off." They got out of the wagon and took the long walk around the store to the loading docks.

They found two men hard at work ripping apart a number of huge foam cartons. Without looking up, one of them—a beefy, red-faced, red-haired type—said, "We don't open for another hour," and kept on working. His partner, a gawky kid with a false front tooth that he popped nervously in and out of place, froze with a piece of carton in each hand and looked at Ben and Jeremy as if they were naked. Jeremy was annoyed enough to want to ask False Tooth what his problem was—after all, they were only wearing what everyone in Arrowsmith wore: faded denim jeans, colorful jackets stuffed with down, and wool hats. Ben was even wearing all his jewelry, as Jeremy would have, had he known the trip was so special.

"We came to talk to Ed Kelleher," Ben told the redhead.

The man looked up, then said to False Tooth, "Go see if Janet's come in yet." He wiped his hands on the front of his yellow coveralls. To Jeremy the suit didn't look terribly warm or comfortable. "You must be from that commune over toward Elkader—what do you call it . . . Arrowsmith, right? I'm Red Hoerner." He extended his hand.

Ben shook with him. "Ben Clayton. This is my boy, Jeremy."

Red nodded and got back to work. "Hell of a cool morning, ain't it? Did you walk down here?"

"We drove," Jeremy said, pleased with his own assertiveness. "Our wagon's out front."

"Oh yeah, that's right: you've got horses and stuff." Red grinned. "Well, I'll say this for those sonsabitches, at least they don't break down. I've got this Chrysler Electric—belonged to my old man and it must be thirty-five years old—and that damned thing might as well be a lawn chair for all the use I get out of it. Power system's been shot for years. Of course, you can't get parts these days. Probably never did work quite right. And you can't drive very far, anyway, unless you want some Blue Meanies for company." The fat man's fingers peeled brown packing material away from something called an Amana Space Furnace. No sooner was the device fully exposed than a piece of it fell off, clanging loudly on the dock. "Well built," Red said, picking up the unit.

"Seems like there's a lot of soldiers around," Ben said.

"No fooling. I guess some outlaws hit a Martin convoy down toward Waterloo last Wednesday. Shot a couple of people and took two whole trucks full of meal. Burned the rest, too. The CSA laid down martial law for the whole county—at least that's what it says on the radio. Nothing's moving on the roads except military vehicles."

Ben nodded. "We saw one of their tricars."

Red laughed. "You saw what? I'm sorry, man, but someone's been filling you full of smoke, if they told you the CSA's flying tricars. Now, they *do* have choppers—"

"We saw a tricar," Jeremy insisted, annoyed that the man didn't seem to believe Ben.

Ben spat off the dock. "Well . . . it was a car and was flying through the air on four fans."

"Then maybe you did, though I'm damned if I know what a machine like that would be doing around here. The Texans are still making 'em so I suppose you might find one, oh, say, in Chicago." He straightened up. "Speaking of Chicago, that's probably where Kenny decided to go. Hey, Kenny!"

Kenny—False Tooth—was on his way back to the dock. With him was a stocky woman in jeans and a sweatshirt. She was about fifty years old and wore glasses with thin blue lenses. "Hello, I'm Janet Kelleher. Ed's wife." She sounded friendlier than she looked. "You're Ben Clayton, aren't you? Ed talked about you a lot. In fact, I think we even met once, about four or five years ago."

Ben nodded as if he found it difficult to talk. Considering the circumstances of their visit, Jeremy understood his reluctance. "We were hoping to have a word with Ed, if we might. Is he going to be around later this morning?"

Janet Kelleher blinked behind her blue lenses and frowned. "I'm sorry to have to tell you this, Ben, but Ed died three weeks ago. He was in a convoy coming back from Dubuque, there was a raid and— well, you know what a temper he had. He got himself shot." She gave a small shrug and tried to smile. "I think, at least, that he went the way he wanted to go—fighting all the way. Now, I suppose you've come with a wagon—"

"We can come back another time, Mrs. Kelleher," Ben said flatly.

"Oh, nonsense, Ben. I can haggle as well as Ed ever did—better, in fact. I ran a branch of the First Iowa Bank over in Oelwein before we were married." She paused. "I've been doing the store's books ever since."

She added a certain emphasis to the phrase which seemed to convince Ben. "Can we go inside?" he asked.

"Of course. Say, where's your wagon?"

"Out front," he said, motioning for Jeremy to follow along. They went into the building through the back door.

"How are you handling this horrible weather up there in the hills?"

"Same as ever," Ben said. "We don't do much, once it gets cold."

He unzipped his jacket. It was warm in here. "Actually, Mrs. Kelleher, we aren't doing too well these days."

She turned and looked at them. "Go on."

Ben didn't look away and didn't rush the words. "You know about the flooding last spring and that hot weather all through August . . . well, it just cut our crops this year to nothing. We've got some stores, of course, but the last three or four years have been pretty thin, too. We don't have much of anything besides corn."

It hurt Jeremy to hear Ben talking like that, all the worse because it was so true. Yes, they had some stores of corn—that was the only crop they could still grow without proper machinery and fertilizers, with no power.

"Now, you know we've always supported ourselves completely," Ben went on. "When we've needed things we couldn't make, we've come down here to trade straight up. And if you'll excuse my saying so, Ed seemed to like everything we brought him." Especially if Ben sneaked it past a CSA patrol, Jeremy thought. "But now it looks like we'll need some big help if we're going to get through the winter."

"I thought this was an unusual time for a visit," Mrs. Kelleher said. The people of Arrowsmith got little craft work, or work on anything for trade, done during harvest. Most of those items were produced when snow covered the ground and days were short. "Did you bring anything at all?"

"The wagon's empty."

She shook her head sadly. "I don't know . . . tell you what, Ben: come up to the office for a minute and let's talk. And for heaven's sake, bring your wagon around to the dock. You don't have to hide it."

As she started up the stairs, Ben told Jeremy, "Go get the wagon."

"Can I do anything to help?" He wanted to be a part of the big negotiation.

"Yeah, get the wagon."

He left Jeremy standing in the doorway, a bit stung.

The lights had come on inside the store. Out front one of Kelleher's clerks was folding the bars back from the windows. Seeing the woman reentering the store through the big double doors inspired

Jeremy to take that route back to the wagon. He walked into the showroom.

He drifted down the main aisle with all the urgency of a leaf in the breeze, head turning from side to side as he passed the televisions, desktop microprocessors, appliances, bright boxes, clothes he wouldn't be caught dead wearing. There were some familiar sights: shiny farm tools, and a rack of rifles that took up a whole corner. But most of the other items were recognizable to him only because he had seen pictures or read about them in the books that Dan kept down at New House. The accumulation was so great that Jeremy thought he would go crazy trying to sort it all out. But while his mind rebelled, his feet carried him outside.

Unable to walk again, he turned and pressed his face to the window, looking back inside. The extra barrier between his eyes and the insane variety of the store allowed him to be a little less dazzled. Nevertheless, he would have given up a free hot meal for a chance to learn exactly what these marvelous machines were for, and how they worked. He looked from one end of the store to the other in search of more identifiable shapes—and found one: a three-bladed rotor the size of a tall man.

It couldn't be! Right here in this store, among everything else, was a rotor for a wind generator.

That was enough to draw him back to the door. He *had* to have a look at this. The two generators in Arrowsmith had been silent as long as he could remember, broken and never fixed, because no one knew how. Jeremy had pored over the old operating manual as if it were *Walden Two,* or *Ecotopia.* He even knew the brand names by now.

Ben and the wagon were forgotten. Jeremy took a deep breath and approached the doors, which promptly slid aside with a faint hiss. He fetched up against a second barrier, a waist-high gate, which did not open automatically.

He was suddenly aware of the bright lights and noise here. He pushed on the gate. It remained closed.

"Please use your Citizen's Card." A voice spoke to him from the ceiling. When he tilted his head back he could see a small metal grill up there.

He touched the gate one more time.

"We remind you that for entry to Kelleher's you *must* use your Citizen's Card. Please insert in the green slot to your right. Thank you." The pleasant voice had grown more insistent. It disturbed Jeremy that he couldn't tell if it belonged to a man or a woman.

"I don't have a Citizen's Card," he told the ceiling. He turned abruptly and ran smack into the outer door which had closed behind him. Feeling like a complete fool now, he decided to wait, quite sure that every person inside the store was having a good laugh. Presently he stepped toward the door again. This time it opened for him.

He hurried toward the wagon.

West Union was awake now, alive with more people than Jeremy had ever seen in one place. Some of them rode by on triped or moped bikes, others drove tiny electric cars. Twice he saw big trucks roll past carrying CSA soldiers. He waited for a collision, if not between two vehicles, then between any vehicle and one of the dozen pedestrians, but nothing happened. He could have watched the maneuvers all day, but people were starting to look at him as he stood there on the sidewalk, his mouth hanging open.

The horse, at least, took it all in stride. Of course, Jeremy reminded himself, she was veteran of numerous trips to West Union. He talked to her a little as he climbed into the seat, then set her off toward the rear of the store.

The wagon rolled past a number of houses that bordered on the Kelleher lot, and Jeremy was beginning to think that in some ways, West Union was a lot more primitive than Arrowsmith. For example, once you got away from the main street you noticed how pitted and lumpy the parking lot really was. Nor were the houses themselves any noticeable improvement over those in the Hill commune. There was more color to them, of course, and they seemed to be in better repair, but even to Jeremy's inexperienced eye the "superiority" was strictly for looks. Why, these houses had no solar panels on their roofs, they were built facing every which way—and all above ground, too—and there wasn't a windmill in sight. Where were the gardens and the smokehouses? Where did the water come from? Did they have electricity? Why did they waste so much house on just two or three people when some slight improvements in design would allow each structure to house three or four times as many. Where did they get all their food?

Don't be stupid, he thought, disgusted at his own ignorance. In West Union they probably had underground pipes for water, wires bringing electricity from miles away, and if they wanted food they just walked over to Kelleher's. No one in Arrowsmith had money. Worse yet, no one had anything to trade anymore—and still all Dan Aucheron and the old crowd could do was get tight-lipped at the mention of "begging the Outsiders for help," and moan about their tough luck. The best idea they had come up with was to send Ben down here to make a deal with Ed Kelleher and hope that, somehow, the gods of the New Age—or better yet, a good spring season— would turn things around.

And if pigs had wings . . .

Jeremy steered the wagon between a pair of produce trucks that were parked behind Kelleher's supermarket section. The smell of fresh bread hung thick in the air, and it made Jeremy's stomach do a little turn.

What if Ben couldn't make a deal?

"Over here, kid!"

Red was shouting at him from beyond the trucks. He guided Jeremy between them and right up to the dock.

"Yeah, there you go. Just let it rest there for a minute. I guess you've got a load of groceries coming, right?"

"If you say so. Need some help?" He wanted to get the goods and be off before anyone changed his mind.

"No need. Kenny and me'll be bringing the stuff when it's ready. Just hold on." He disappeared into the store again, passing Ben, who approached the wagon with a satisfied look on his face.

"What did you say to her?" Jeremy asked.

"I didn't have to say much. We've done a lot of business for the store over the years, so I suppose she was glad to help us out a bit. Of course," he added, smiling thinly, "I don't think she'd have been quite as anxious to help us out if that other business had been more on the legal side. I guess the CSA is really cracking down on the dope and the black market around here."

Jeremy cleared his throat. "Uh, do you think she'd give us any-thing else, since she's feeling generous today?"

Ben sighed. "What is it now, Jeremy?"

"Out in the front they've got the kind of rotors that we need to get the generators working again—"

Ben was shaking his head at the mention of generators. "Damn it, Jeremy, are you still worrying about those things? Can you ever leave well enough alone? I'm sorry, but no. We'll probably need whatever credit we have left over."

He wasn't going to give up that easily. "Hey, Red," he called. "What would it take to get me one of those Sencenbaugh rotors you have?"

Red swung a dolly loaded with boxes to a stop at the lip of the dock. "Well, they run about two thousand dollars new—"

"*Jeremy* . . ." Ben said tiredly. "Two thousand dollars?"

"We *need* something like this, Ben!" The words were out before he could stop them, even though he knew Ben was more tolerant of his ideas than anyone else.

"Maybe someday, but this isn't the biggest problem we have. You know that. Now, next spring . . ."

"I just keep thinking how this is the one thing that keeps us living like a bunch of cavemen. If we *had* electricity, we'd have lights at night, we wouldn't have to do everything by day—"

"That's enough!" Ben hissed. "Jeremy, you don't know point one about doing business down here. No matter what *good* it would do, that rotor costs more than this whole load of food multiplied by five. You tell me which is more important. Then, if you're still dumb enough to be arguing, you tell me where you're going to get money, because that's what you're going to need."

"Hey, you guys," Hoerner said, "I can get you a rotor, if that's what you're looking for."

"Where?" Jeremy wanted to know.

"Would it be okay?" Red asked Ben. "It'd be *free.*"

"Show him, if you want to," Ben said. "He's the expert."

"Hey, Kenny," Red hollered. "Finish this up, will you? Come with me, kid."

They jumped off the dock, dodged through the trucks and into an alley that opened between the two nearest houses. "It's not far," Red told him.

The sky had grown cloudy, making a liar out of the earlier sunshine. Jeremy knew that the day had gotten as warm as it would get. It was actually cold in the alley.

He followed Hoerner until they were behind some of the Main Street stores. Red stopped in front of a rickety shed. "It's been a while since I saw it, but there used to be an old rotor laying around here. I think they'd practically pay you to haul it away."

"How do you know that?"

"My brother's the one who threw the thing away, that's why."

"Is there something wrong with it?"

"I don't think so. He sold the place where he was living, out east of town, a few years ago. The Martin people wanted the land. They didn't have any use for a peewee generator, of course, so Ray yanked the rotor off the tower when he moved." Hoerner tugged at the shed's door and found it locked. "Let me see if he's around. I'll be back in a second." He left Jeremy alone at the shed.

It was a long, green plastic structure that looked as though it would fold in the first strong wind, but it was obvious that the shed had survived for a lot of years: vines covered one whole side and a number of tall trees grew close behind it.

"Okay, kid." Cigarette in his mouth, Red Hoerner appeared beside him, a key jangling in his hand. "Let's see what we've got in the old shed here." He fumbled with the lock.

The door opened. The interior of the shed was cluttered and dark, and seemed to contain nothing but moldy cardboard boxes piled in no particular order. "There we go," Red said, pointing to a dusty shape leaning against one wall.

The rotor was at least half a yard taller than Jeremy and would surely be awkward to handle, but two strong people could manage it. What he was most concerned about, however, was the eventual fitting. When wind generators had first come into use there had been dozens of competing types on the market, and few had parts that were compatible with the others. The generators raised at Arrowsmith for Hill House and New House were Sencenbaughs, the brand most suited to the local climate and mean wind speed. And as he scraped the accumulated dust off the head he saw a dim "S" logo. "I think it'll work," he told Red.

"Okay, then, how do you want to move it?"

"It's big, but it's not very heavy." That, at least was what all the old manuals had said.

"You're the boss." The two men tugged the rotor outside and leaned it against the shed. "Hold it for a minute," Red said, reaching for the door, which had swung wide open. "What the hell is *that?*" He was looking around the corner.

There was a tricar parked in the alley.

Up close it was as big as one of the armored CSA trucks he had seen earlier, vaguely cylindrical, if you pictured a cylinder that looked pregnant in the middle and flat on the ends. The vehicle rested on four fat tires at the moment; its fans were retracted and tucked underneath. The whole thing looked about as natural here in a West Union alley as a weasel in a henhouse, and Jeremy fell instantly in love.

"Do you think I could look at it?" Jeremy said.

"What, the car?" Hoerner shrugged. "Go ahead. Let me lock up."

Hesitantly, Jeremy went up to the tricar and stretched out a hand, afraid that if he used the wrong touch the car might shy away like a spooked horse. But the metal skin was still, cool, and smooth, seeming to throb with power and strength. He couldn't help from laughing out loud. Wow!

There was something funny about the windows, though. They looked like mirrors from a distance, but when you got right up to them you could see inside. Jeremy shielded his eyes and looked— there was the front seat . . . the *cockpit,* that was what it was called . . . every bit as spectacular as he'd imagined it, with its steering tiller and dash instruments, including a screen which had lighted numbers scrolling even now. From this angle the back seat was blocked from view, so he edged around to the rear for a look there—

An inhuman face peered back at him.

Was it an animal? A shape that might have been an arm reached toward the window. Jeremy fell over getting away from the car. He bumped right into Hoerner.

"Hey!" He had just closed the door. He plucked the cigarette out of his mouth. "I wonder where this baby came from?"

Jeremy glanced at the tricar. The face was gone, and whatever he had seen remained hidden behind the tricar's windows, which now gleamed like a wall of silver. Had he been dreaming?

No, his imagination didn't run to snaky arms and animal faces. He had actually seen a creature that was not a human being, or, at least, not a healthy one. The face had a snout like a dog's and slit eyes that ran from ear to ear—if you could call things that looked like bat wings ears. The "arm" itself had been odd, coiling the way it did.

"When we saw it this morning it was coming from the southwest."

"That don't narrow it down too much." The fat man walked to the rear of the car, keeping his distance. He stuck the cigarette back in his mouth. "Doesn't look like it's been here long, that's for sure. Someone just drove in the back way, parked it and left. Wonder who?"

"Someone in town?"

"Are you kidding? I told you, nobody around here's got *anything* like this. I don't think they even sell them in the CSA. And if you had one you sure wouldn't be able to afford to buy fuel for it. Goddamn, *you* people would be just as likely to have one of these things as I would." Hoerner leaned toward the window. "It sure is a nice-looking piece of machinery, though—"

"Hey . . ."

Hoerner glanced at Jeremy and grinned. "Don't worry, I won't touch anything."

"Ah . . . there's someone in the back seat."

The fat man straightened up slowly. "Well, why the hell didn't you tell me that?" He smiled once more and waved pleasantly in the general direction of the car's back seat.

"I'm sorry," Jeremy said, swallowing. "It's just—I never saw anybody who looked like that before."

Hoerner stared at him. "What are you talking about, kid?"

"Look in the back seat."

He did, after a moment's hesitation, and didn't stay put long enough to cast a shadow, his head snapping back like he'd been punched. He turned pale. "Let's get that prop and get out of here!"

"What is it?"

"Just get moving—here." Hoerner grabbed two of the rotor vanes while Jeremy took the third. The rotor was heavy, but they could carry it as long as Jeremy steadied his end, which included the core. He had to walk backward to do the job properly.

They hadn't gone a dozen steps when Hoerner told him, "Stop right there."

A young woman in a baggy green outfit topped by a patterned cape was headed their way. She pulled a Kelleher's shopping cart that was piled high with paper bags full of groceries, and she seemed to be in a big hurry.

As she passed she gave them a stare. She had curly black hair done up in some kind of braid, a broad, well-tanned face, and dark eyes. Jeremy knew without asking that she was the owner of the mysterious tricar.

The woman took a few more steps, then turned abruptly. They were still watching her. "Is there something I can do for you guys?" Her words had a funny sound to them, so funny, in fact, that Jeremy almost failed to understand them.

"No, thanks," Hoerner said. "We were just leaving."

"See you around then, okay?"

Hoerner nodded, and nudged Jeremy into motion. As he backed down the alley the strange woman disappeared around the corner of the shed. The heavy sounds of the tricar's doors being opened and slammed shut echoed off the old brick walls. "It's hers all right," Red said. "I wonder what a Texan is doing up in these parts?"

So that was it. Even in Arrowsmith you could hear about Texas, which had been the strongest region of the old United States, and how it had gobbled up most of the American Southwest and parts of Mexico in the War. Only a Texan would own a machine like a tricar. "She's a long way from home," Jeremy said.

"No kidding." Hoerner frowned. "Listen, you seem to be a fairly bright guy, so pay attention. I don't know what's going on around here so it might be best for both of us to keep our mouths shut about Miss Houston there *and* her car—and the *passenger*. I smell blue coats all over this already, and I don't want them chasing after me, too. Got that?"

"Sure," Jeremy said. "What was in the car?" Hoerner would be more familiar with strange creatures than someone from up in the hills.

"You really don't know?" Hoerner shook his head. "No, I suppose you wouldn't. Well, Jeremy, you just saw a Hocq in person—just your average, everyday alien being from another planet. I've never seen one that close before but they've been all over the TV for years. Crazy bastards, too."

Jeremy recognized the name now. Hocq. Hawk. Ben had picked it up on one of his trips years ago.

There was no chance for further questions. They had reached the wagon where Ben was waiting patiently. He helped them lay the rotor across the wagon bed and lash it down. Two of the vanes stuck out to the sides and the third hung out the rear.

"Let's get going," Ben said, climbing aboard. Jeremy could tell that he wasn't happy.

Hoerner slapped him on the shoulder. "See you later, kid. Drop by some other time." He added quietly, "And remember what I told you."

"Don't worry." He would remember: How could he forget?

He steered the wagon back to the street.

"Turn left instead of right," Ben told him. "We'll have to take the south road."

"Why the long way around?"

"Horse can't pull uphill all day with a heavy load." There was an edge to Ben's voice that discouraged further discussion. And the tricky business of crossing a city street at the helm of a horse-drawn wagon kept Jeremy fully occupied for the next half hour, until they were well clear of West Union. This road was far better maintained than Highway 56, but there was still no real traffic. As they rounded the last bend out of town, they saw why.

Half a dozen blue-coated CSA troopers had set up a roadblock. Already one of them was motioning for Jeremy to slow down.

Ben looked even more unhappy. "What's the problem?" he called to the soldiers.

Jeremy brought the wagon to a complete stop. "Get out," one of the soldiers said simply. They got out.

This soldier wore a helmet that covered his head from eyebrows to collarbone. It was blue, like the heavy coat, though most of the paint had peeled or was hidden under caked dirt. The soldier's eyes were hidden behind dark goggles. "Where are you going?"

"Down the road about ten miles, then west about six more," Ben replied. "If you'll let us."

The soldier didn't seem to hear. There were still five more hovering around a truck parked to the side of the highway. The roadblock itself was nothing fancy, just two orange sawhorses that straddled the traffic lanes.

"What you got in the back?" The soldier tapped the side of the wagon with his rifle barrel.

"Food," Ben said.

"And a rotor," Jeremy added.

The soldier poked the barrel under the rotor, lifting the tarp that covered their groceries.

"Doesn't look like machine guns to me," said a second soldier, who had come up to the wagon on the other side. This soldier was so small he had to stand on tiptoe just to see into the back. Apparently satisfied, the second soldier stood back and pushed up his goggles. Jeremy was surprised to see that this soldier was female. He never thought of CSA soldiers as anything but faceless men. "Let them be," she said.

"Yeah," said a third. "They're just Hook and Eye Dutch or something, right?" He grinned at Ben and Jeremy. Ben smiled back.

The first soldier had secured the tarp again. "Sorry to bother you," he said. He raised his goggles, too, and was revealed to be younger than Jeremy.

"Are you looking for outlaws?" Jeremy asked, bolder now that he had seen the ordinary faces behind the fearsome masks.

"We're *always* looking for outlaws," the youngest soldier said. He moved to pull aside the roadblock, thus ending the conversation. Jeremy urged the horse along.

They were about a half a mile away before he said anything to Ben. "How long is all that going to last?"

"The food? About five or six weeks, if we're careful."

For the first time since leaving Kelleher's Jeremy noticed that all of Ben's rings were gone. So *that* was the deal . . .

He thought again of the constant pain in his gut, and recalled that he had not had anything to eat today except tea. He wanted to close his eyes and make the pain go away, make the winter go away. Anyway, Ben's jewelry had bought them some time. They would eat well for six weeks.

Winter was four months long.

CHAPTER 4

Outlaw Territory, Monday Afternoon

Lisa Marquez knew that she was a lot smarter today than she was yesterday. She would never, ever get involved in anything like this again.

In the space of less than fourteen hours she had made three potentially fatal—if unavoidable—mistakes, which did not bode well for the rest of their trip.

After borrowing the keys from Shapiro on the pretext that she'd left her briefing cassette in the tricar, she had been able to sneak Harrek into the back seat of the Oberheim Hurricane, one of the three cruisers carried by the mission and specially modified to move the Hocq from place to place. There was no trouble. The guards at the Hilton were there to prevent the unruly populace from getting to the aliens and their escorts, not the other way around, so she was able to drive out of the garage unquestioned, even though it was after dark.

But the original plans called for a rendezvous at television station KMGH in Denver, where it was hoped the glare of immediate public exposure would keep the Texans and African mother hens from reacting violently to Harrek's defection. The trouble was, Lisa's contact could not be in Denver until Thursday. Thus she spent precious minutes standing in a public phone at Pulaski and Cermak before realizing the utter futility of trying to call California from the People's Republic without blowing her contact's cover and her own location. They had not had time for drops or prearranged signals or other tools of spycraft; they were all amateurs. Parking a very conspicuous Oberheim Hurricane in front of a public phone booth had endangered everything and gained nothing. Mistake number one.

Her second came on the flight itself.

For five hours she hedge-hopped the Hurricane across the plains of northern Illinois south of Rockford, then zigzagged close to the Wisconsin border. She worried more about her ability to control the cruiser than the need to outrun patrols; the Hurricane had great thrust and military-style guidance, having been a Ranger prowl in Fort Worth before modifications. She flew with eyes on the readouts and the windows, and with one ear tuned to the fuzzbuster (which squealed every time it came into contact with People's Republic radars) and the other monitoring various public and official frequencies for news of their "escape." She heard nothing at all—which surprised her, but only at first.

North of Galena, over Wisconsin, she dipped into the bluff country, slowing to ground-car speeds in order to slip safely between the fire zones of the forts on the People's Republic side of the Mississippi and the Central States installations on the opposite bank. That was relatively easy, since Chicago and the CSA were currently in a state of détente and thus on low alert status. The problem came in simply getting across the damned river.

She put down on the water, hoping to chug straight to the other side, then drive up the bluffs into Iowa and relative safety. But she learned a lesson that river pilots had learned the hard way for two hundred years: you can't trust the Mississippi. The cruiser smacked into a submerged bar and to get free Lisa was forced to spin up the forward fans. She got free of the bar at the cost of a fouled and useless number three fan.

The Hurricane could fly with three, but not too well and not too fast, and certainly not for eight hundred miles, which unfortunately happened to be the distance between this part of Iowa and Denver.

She stayed on the beach until dawn. At first light she edged the cruiser into the sky on three fans and limped inland, drifting northwest to avoid the Dubuque traffic zone, looking for a safe place to set down. She and Harrek would need food, for one thing, as well as rest —and somewhere to hide while she repaired the fan. If it could be repaired.

Somewhere turned out to be a smallish town called West Union about twenty-five miles inland from the Mississippi. She was rolling through its back streets less than an hour after lifting off from the beach.

That was her third mistake.

She stashed the Hurricane—and Harrek—in an alley behind a good-sized supermarket, where she used the last of her People's Republic dollars (thanking God for détente and currency exchange) to buy food and basic camping gear. She wanted to buy fuel bricks, but doubted they would be available without local ration coupons, if they were available at all. She returned to find two local yokels poking around the car. It was likely that the nosy bastards saw Harrek. She could only hope that their story, sure to be told at the nearest bar, wouldn't be believed until she and the alien were long gone from here.

She hoped. And so she drove out of town, taking to the air once safely outside city limits, heading southeast, into the hills, into what her guidance system optimistically labeled "Unregulated Land."

At least here in this near-wilderness, outside the zones of government influence, they would be momentarily safe from the prying eyes of Great Texas. And not only Texas, but Banekker's Africans and the Soviets and the Easterners . . . all of them skilled, equipped, suspicious, and desperate for the Genesis material. If she could give those monsters the slip, she shouldn't have too much trouble hiding out in the CSA for a few days. One thing was certain: she could not turn back. That unpleasant thought had the virtue of focusing her thinking. They had to get to sanctuary in California . . .

What a picture that brought to mind! A Special Assistant to the Governor of Great Texas flying into the badlands like some fugitive in a John Ford movie. *Pobre chica!*

She glanced into the rear-view mirror at her passenger. Harrek sat wedged into a collapsible frame that had itself been shoe-horned into the back seat. He looked small and hurt—quite a feat, considering his imposing size. Harrek had a right to feel pain, however. The Hocq had evolved on a world possessing less than two thirds the mass of the Earth; thus Harrek was used to carrying two thirds of his current weight. Lisa recalled how miserable she felt when she gained ten pounds . . .

Toughen up, Lisa. Harrek is the one who decided to roll these dice.

The guidance beeped and she took manual control again, touching her throat mike. "Hold tight, Harrek." She neither saw nor heard a response, and the horrid thought occurred to her: What if he dies?

The land here was rolling, covered with woods, bare fields, countless valleys, and tiny creeks. From her relatively low altitude she counted the ruins of half a dozen farms. She didn't know an awful lot about the history of the area, but she knew it wasn't the collapse or the wars that killed off these farms: they'd been dying for years, gradually giving way to giant agrifactories like those that sprawled to the north of West Union. Yet it saddened her to see these gray, tumbledown barns and broken silos, fields gone back to weed. She wondered about the families that had lived here so long ago. Had they become refugees? Or had they taken to the woods with rifles and jeeps, joined the Aryan Nation or the Posse Comitatus? Become outlaws?

She banked the Hurricane and began to descend. It was near midafternoon now and she had no time to play tourist. They needed a campsite that would afford easy landing and takeoff while protecting them from view.

Oops, too fast! She pulled back on the tiller and the cruiser climbed in response.

From the speaker came a rasping sound. "Sorry, Harrek," she said. At least he's alive! But she was sorry she'd hurt him with that sudden climb.

They swooped over the crest of a low hill, and Lisa got the surprise of her life. Three tiny pillars of smoke curled into the sky from locations not far ahead. Great! The last thing she needed now was to land in the middle of an outlaw camp . . .

But her options were limited at the moment. She eased the Hurricane into another turn and aimed it back at the last ruined farm, trying to convince herself that outlaws never stayed in one place too long, that this was too far north of the main highways they raided. After all, this was the middle of the Central States . . . wheat fields and snowmen, Lisa! Rotten, crumbling little cities holding out their hands for satellite power from California, money from Chicago, oil from Texas. Outlaws and farmers.

Besides, having run off with a member of the first extraterrestrial mission ever to visit Earth she had, in effect, taken on the governments of two planets. Why worry about a bunch of back-country human beings?

She spotted her farm and started down.

CHAPTER 5

Arrowsmith, Tuesday Morning

"Looks like a long climb," Neil Wittek said, standing at the base of the tower and looking up.

"We did it once," Jeremy told him.

"Six years ago."

"That's why it should be a lot easier now. We've already done most of the work."

Five stories tall, the wind machine rose out of the bare field north of Hill House like a fist thrown at the sky. The "arm," the tower itself, consisted of half a dozen eight-sided sections stacked one on top of the other, tapering to the "fist," which was the pod housing the long-dead electric generator.

"I suppose." Neil chewed at the ends of his droopy mustache. He was one of the half-dozen members of the commune near Jeremy's age, and the only boy. He always seemed to have a tough time keeping up. Absently he tugged at a wooden ladder attached to one of the massive tower legs. A piece of it came away in his hands.

Neil just looked at Jeremy.

"Let's get the wagon," Jeremy said tiredly. "This is going to take some time."

"Okay."

After yesterday's adventure in West Union Jeremy had worked through the night on the old batteries in the powerhouse down the hill. It had not been easy work, warming the cells, cleaning the connections, loading them with distilled water hauled all the way from Hugh Walton's rig down at New House, but the presence of the new rotor spurred him on. It was the key element lacking six years ago when he and Neil had spoiled the clean lines of the tower by adding a crude scaffold to it.

"Why don't you drive?" Jeremy suggested. "Back it up to the west face."

Neil climbed aboard, clucking to the horse, while Jeremy leaped into the back to protect the rotor. The wagon swung around slowly to avoid the frozen furrows that ran up to the tower base.

"You know, I can't believe you finally got hold of one of these things," Neil said.

"Neither can I. I wish I could have seen the look on old Dan's face when *he* found out." Dan Aucheron lived down at the larger Sun House with the majority of the community.

"I bet nobody's had the guts to tell him."

It was Dan Aucheron who told them they were wasting their time —community time!—six years ago. "Those machines was never worth a damn," he'd said. "The one at New House got broke when that propeller thing blew off in a tornado and I don't know what happened to the other one at all." Dan neglected to mention that the New House rotor "got broke" because Cissy Funderburk had neglected to feather the machine in the storm. Sure enough, the violent oscillations wrenched the generator pod completely off its tower. The rusted pile of wreckage, now covered with weeds, still lay near New House. As for the missing Hill House rotor, that was a bit of a mystery. Had it been broken? Stolen by outlaws? No one seemed to remember, though Elizabeth told Jeremy she thought it had been deliberately removed, probably for maintenance. If so, the Hill House rotor had never been returned. As long as Jeremy could remember, the generating pod had sat on its tower rotorless and useless.

In their original plans Jeremy and Neil had dreamed of fashioning a whole new rotor out of wood. But that idea had been abandoned when Jeremy found out that a wood rotor would be ripped by pieces by the stress.

Here was his last chance.

They unloaded the rotor at the tower base. To his waist Jeremy strapped a wide, heavy belt salvaged from the old powerhouse. To the belt he attached a hammer, two screwdrivers, a wrench, several sockets, a big C-clamp, and a pulley. He looped rope around his shoulder. He didn't know just how much of this armament was entirely necessary—in fact, he was still unsure of the exact steps he would take to connect the big rotor to the generator's drive shaft, even though he had rehearsed it—but the feel of the tool belt gave him new confidence.

All he had to do now was climb.

He put his weight on the ladder, careful to avoid the rung Neil had damaged. When this failed to dump him on his behind, he started up.

The ladder took him to the base of the first section of the tower. From here he could simply crawl up girders and cross braces, a process which involved considerable twisting and turning. But he quickly established a rhythm and didn't stop to rest until he was two thirds of the way to the top.

At that point he was high enough to look down on the glassy solar panels roofing Hill House—high enough, for that matter, to look the rooster-shaped weathervane atop the barn right in the eye. He had to be sure to keep that 'vane in sight; the wind had been gusting all morning and he didn't want to be leaning the wrong way when it started up again.

He had also drawn a crowd of spectators.

"Jeremy! You be careful up there!"

That was Heather, her swollen shape and red hair easy to recognize even from this height. Playfully, he swung away from the tower and waved, drawing gasps from his small audience, which included not only Heather, but his mother Elizabeth, Cory Turner, and Neil, who was now trudging across the field toward the tower.

"Jeremy, stop that!"

He could see Heather shaking her head and making some comment to Elizabeth, so he quit goofing around and got on with his job. In a few moments he reached the platform which circled the downwind or prop side of the tower about five feet below the generating pod itself.

They had built the platform out of nails and boards salvaged from a ruined farm just up the road. Since the restoration of power was not one of Dan's priorities, they had not been able to draw on community resources. It was just as well: they had been able to work on the platform away from the prying eyes of Dan and his watchdogs. Nevertheless, for a moment Jeremy wondered about that choice. Fresh-cut wood weathered better than wood exposed to air for decades. Six years of rain, sun, and snow might have softened the platform to the consistency of wet cardboard. A foot would go right through, and that would be the end of Jeremy and his project.

Here goes . . . He took the last step, making it a hard one.

The platform was so solid it hurt.

His problems weren't over yet. The platform was actually a frame —Neil called it a "treehouse"—part of which ran up and over the top of the generator pod to permit access to the whole machine, not just the bottom. Jeremy knew that the "treehouse" degraded the pod's aerodynamics and efficiency, since the prop was downwind and thus dependent on the flow of air that reached it for its power. But there was no other way to get at things. Jeremy couldn't just drop the machine to the ground and work on it there.

Half power was better than no power.

He shifted his weight completely to the platform and knelt on the rough planks. Still no telltale creaking and bending. He did not let go of the frame, however, as the wind came up to remind him just how exposed he was.

The uneasiness passed and he stood for the first time.

Six years ago he had left the generator head covered with plastic, and the plastic was still in place . . . filthy and frayed, but whole. He tore it off and let it flutter to the ground. With a wave to Heather and Elizabeth, he swung onto the crude ladder which would get him all the way to the top. A second gust of wind shook the whole tower and he pressed himself flat against the boards until it let up.

Pulling and twisting again, he was able to lock his legs around the supports and reach, finally, for the tools on his belt. He tried to remember the steps. Attach the clamp to the support frame, hang the pulley from the clamp, thread the rope, drop the ends. Then all he would need was a little help from his friends. Thank God the prop was merely big rather than heavy. They could raise it up here with no effort, though Jeremy was ready to use the horse, if necessary. All he really needed was for the rotor to hang in front of the generator shaft head for a couple of seconds . . .

Far below Neil struggled to fasten the rope to the prop. Heather helped, grabbing the free end of the rope, which flapped in the breeze.

When he was finished, Neil shouted, "Okay!" The spectators, true to the spirit of the community, quit watching and helped. Cory and Elizabeth pulled with Neil while Heather steadied.

The rusted pulley squeaked in protest and tiny chips of metal crumbled away as the rope slipped through. A silly grab at it cost Jeremy some skin off the palm of his hand. Nothing he could do here. But, jerkily, the prop rose, banging against the tower from time to time.

Here it was. "Hold it there!" he called. Quickly and carefully—he was leaning a bit far—he tugged the rotor toward the shaft. After a frustrating moment, it slid on. He caught his breath, then reached out to tighten it down. That done, he loosened the rope and crawled away.

Once he was safely back on the platform below the pod he put the generator in gear. He heard a groan, but the rotor turned. He squirted oil into the housing and closed it.

The rotor turned freely in the wind. Jeremy couldn't help smiling. Hill House had lights!

Power to the People!

Worldlines, by their nature, must have beginnings. His had begun at an exclusive spa where the First came for their rashch, high above the Beggar's Plain near the city of Khit on the planet known once simply as the World, now called Shen. (Should he now think of shenlines? In his language it was the same sound.) Worldlines, by their nature, extend, predictably, sensibly . . . through the post-rashch trauma and infancy . . . into school and apprenticeship, gathering strands, twisting, growing through the phases of a life.

What had caused his worldline to vector across the light-years to this planet, for the moment known simply as Earth?

This philosophical question occupied the mind of Harrek al-Khittim, conjugant of Excellency Boroz mi al-Khittim and currently most junior (and, it was said, least reliable) member of the Holy

Mission of the One People—now known as the "Hocq." It took his mind off the pain.

The pain, for the most part, was of a purely physical nature, the logical result of relocating from one's relatively harmonious native environment to one characterized by, among other things, a gravity half again as strong as is decent. Harrek regretted his own dismissal of that single horrible factor upon its suggestion to him prior to the Mission's launch those many seasons ago. Combine the brutal gravity of this Earth's environment with an atmosphere whose chemical components would support a member of the People only if he chose to remain very still and semiconscious (and ignoring, for the moment, the millions of trace substances, chemical and organic, to which the Hocq were highly allergic) and you produce a situation that only the most heroic or unlucky member of the First Caste would tolerate.

Harrek was not a First.

This was also a source of pain: Harrek was not of the First Caste and, following this latest escapade, might never be. Nonetheless, he was quite aware of the duties and privileges of that high station. It was this discrepancy between his actual and desired status that motivated Harrek's escape from captivity (for that was how he had come to perceive his membership in the Hocq mission). Prior to that escape, the question of Harrek's ascent—which could be accomplished only by rashch, and rashch accomplished only with the cessation of certain medical treatment, and cessation of said treatment impossible within the reach of Boroz—awaited a great number of what the People were wont to refer to as "fortunate deaths." In Harrek's case, this number was quite high . . . though not, perhaps, quite high enough to justify Boroz's acid estimate of "six times six times six."

The escape, at least, would force the issue. Harrek would never be Second again. He would be First, or he would demonstrate another principle . . . worldlines, by their nature, must end.

Nevertheless, at this point on his worldline, aching, his ears drooping, his greater arms bruised, Harrek dwelled on the latter, more mathematically likely, possibility.

He examined his motives and found that the rugged voyage across the wilderness had somewhat dulled their shine. This was one of the most primitive parts of an already primitive world. Even the Earthers themselves admitted it. In such a place he would find little comfort in his hour of need.

He rested in a tiny pressure tent that he and his companion had carried aboard their escape vehicle. There would not have been room for him to stand, since it was an Earther construct. Even in a semireclined position, however, he might have been able to spread both sets of arms to the fullest—how he longed to do that!—had the tent's interior not been taken up with a portable compressor, air bottles, a sleeping rack, and, perhaps most important of all, his pressurized sortie suit.

Well, he was too sore to perform any decent exercises anyway. He ate.

Presently he felt strong enough to don the rigid suit, which was necessary if he wanted to take a single step in an uncontrolled Earther environment. (He had grown to love Earther hotels, since in them suits were not always required!) His senses told him that the sun had set. His ears were quite sensitive to changes in background noise, and the sounds he heard—filtering, of course, through the constant noise of the compressor—were those of night: a wind of sorts, occasional snorts and snuffles from four-legged creatures that prowled nearby, the evening cries of tiny winged creatures passing overhead on what must be a long voyage toward warmer climates. Harrek felt almost comfortable on Earth at night because of these sounds, so reminiscent to those of the Beggar's Plain, and also because his eyes were better able to function without light than those of Earthers. In darkness, therefore, he was not at such a disadvantage compared to the natives.

With relative ease—he could move somewhat gracefully in the pressure suit now, after years of practice—he opened the inner tent flap, exiting into the narrow chamber beyond. He closed the flap behind, and switched on the compressor. His companion had told him this tent was like those used by Earthers exploring the fourth planet of this solar system, where the biosphere was more dangerous to them than was Earth's to the Hocq. Harrek admired the Earthers' ability to place faith in such flimsy constructs.

He opened the outer flap and, with great snapping and stamping sounds, caused his suit to propel him into the yard.

There was their escape vehicle, where they had landed it, with one of its forward propelling units in pieces. A fire flickered nearby. Looking toward it momentarily overloaded the suit's optics. Harrek turned away.

They were camped on a flat patch of bare ground and gravel studded, Harrek perceived, with dead vegetation undoubtedly dormant due to the extreme thermal gradient experienced at this latitude in this season.

There were two, possibly three, dead buildings nearby as well. One appeared to have been a food-storage construct, but the roof was missing and there were openings in its sides. Harrek had made detailed studies of the architectural habits of Earthers of this continent; they would not build a storage structure without a roof. Therefore this particular building was in serious disrepair. He noted a second structure which did not yield itself to speculative reconstruction, perhaps because only its overgrown rectangular foundation survived.

However, it was the third structure, an obvious dwelling, which fascinated Harrek. He did not need his training in Earther customs to know this, for the building had that sloppy, unfinished look which is characteristic of the "homes" of many intelligent species. Here was a partial construct added to the central building at a later date. Here were signs of renovation and improvement in the basic design (though none recently). The home seemed strong and secure and no doubt its walls still echoed with the voices of its long-vanished inhabitants.

Harrek wished they would return. His projections of success in this particular venture—the escape—depended upon his ability to contact as many different Earthers of varying ethnic and economic caste as possible.

He heard the approaching footfalls of his companion before she spoke. "Harrek! What are you doing out here?"

He rotated the walking suit. Lisa Marquez came toward him with an armload of dead vegetation. He did not question her right to demand justification for his actions. As an Earther, on Earth, her caste was higher than his . . . higher even than a First.

He activated his speaking system, making an effort as well to form sounds in his companion's language, which he had studied since the mission began. "I wanted to look around."

Lisa dropped the pile of branches and began adding them to the fire. "Don't get too fond of this place. With a little luck we'll be out of here in a day or two." She wrapped her arms around herself as if cold, a curiously Hocq-like gesture. "Besides, it's kind of creepy here."

"How is it creepy here? This is not a jungle. Most of the creatures within my perception limits walk as you and I."

"Jokes, yet." She stood up. "I'm sorry. It's been a long day. How are you feeling, anyway?"

"Well enough, considering the circumstances."

"I'll be the first to admit that the ride left a lot to be desired."

"It was quite satisfactory," Harrek said, quite sincerely. "Especially when examined in view of the alternatives."

As Harrek spoke Lisa went about preparing herself for sleep. They had not been able to bring a tent-construct for her, so she would have to make herself comfortable, if possible, in the cruiser. Harrek did not envy her, especially since it was obvious that she was exhausted. He could not help but feel a sense of affection for her and her efforts —as if she were his own conjugant!—so strong as to make him want to dance. The encumbering suit prevented any such display. Just as well: Lisa would probably find it frightening.

His great elation, of course, was matched by his glee at the position in which he had left his dear conjugant, Boroz. The Ambassador was surely in a classic rage, threatening the other long-suffering Hocq, and, naturally, whatever poor humans came into her range. Her own conjugant run away! Secrets of the People spilled indiscriminately! The search abandoned! The Mission betrayed!

"There we go," Lisa said, stepping back to admire her work.

"You have previous experience in the wilderness?"

"Lots. Eight weeks of Basic and a couple of weekends with the state militia." She shook her head. "No, I'm afraid I'm as new to this game as you are."

"Then your complicity is all the more to be wondered at."

She laughed.

"May one ask a question?"

"One may," she said.

"When I first approached you to arrange an informal meeting with citizens of California, why did you not . . . report me?"

"Why, because there was nothing to report. It was a perfectly justifiable request and I was the logical person to whom to make it. One of my titles is . . . *was* . . . Special Assistant for Western Affairs." She did not look at him but rather gazed up into the dark night sky of Earth. Harrek would have to be satisfied with her answer. Though her words delivered a clear message, there was something in her tone which he could not immediately categorize. "May I ask a question?"

"You may."

"Why did you approach me? There were other candidates you could have chosen. You were seeing people from California all the time!"

"You are a Texan and thus less likely to be under suspicion."

"And?"

"I was able to learn that you had been born in Anaheim." Harrek paused. "California."

Now Lisa was looking at him. "You're saying that I was obviously disloyal?"

"No. I would say that you were obviously ambitious."

She laughed out loud. "I didn't know the Hocq had such skill with non sequitur. You're going to have to explain that to me someday."

"Yes, it will be time for frank and open exchange of information."

Lisa got herself into a Hocq-like posture and executed a creditable Hocq gesture of farewell between members of equal caste. "Good night, Harrek." She ducked into the car and closed the door.

Harrek was still intrigued with Lisa's willingness to become involved with his plan. He was certain that because of Boroz's countless humiliations and the struggle with the physicians over the anti-rashch drugs he had been clinically insane when he proposed it to her in the first place. And when the conference in Los Angeles had been canceled, he had been certain that the escape was canceled, and that he would be trapped forever.

But this Earther had kept her promise. Perhaps *she* was the one for whom Boroz and, indeed, the entire Mission searched?

And Harrek the lesser had stolen her away!

Such thoughts, and their place on his worldline, deserved further contemplation. As the stars brightened in their unfamiliar places, Harrek commanded his suit to a fully upright position and began to walk toward the perimeter of their camp. For a moment he was seized by an unfamiliar feeling, one hinting of vertigo, but it passed, and he remained alert, awake, prepared to seize the means of his ascent, here, in California, or anywhere.

CHAPTER 6

Arrowsmith, Tuesday Night

It was the first party they'd had in years. It was the first time Ben had said the blessing in years:

"Respect the principles, reject the establishment. Christianity without Christians, communism without Communists, conservation without governments." He looked up and smiled. "Let's eat."

The fourteen residents of Hill House, with the exception of Hugh Walton, who had to chop wood down at Sun House, were gathered in the dining room to thank Ben and Jeremy. The meal was plain— potato flakes, beans, and something resembling beef—but the mood was special. Women and men dressed in their finest, an old linen cloth on the table, Ben laughing at one of Neil's jokes. And there was light in the House.

Last night there had been no special welcome for Ben and Jeremy upon their return, though everyone was impressed and pleased at the results of their trip. That was how it was done in Arrowsmith: no job was more important than any other. But most of those who lived in Hill House knew the importance of that trip. They used Jeremy's new lights as an excuse to thank both men. Maybe they *would* make it, Jeremy thought. Maybe they would stay together . . .

"Oh, and Brandy Kramer came by just before dinner," Elizabeth said. "She thinks there's something strange going on at the old Quiller farm."

"Brandy Kramer says there's something strange going on *everywhere,*" Jeremy said, to general laughter.

"Brandy is part of this community, too," Ben said quietly, effectively reminding Jeremy that his attitude was inappropriate for this evening.

"Sorry," Jeremy said, looking to Heather for forgiveness and receiving only a look of mild reproach in return. More than once Brandy Kramer had invited all of them to Sun House to "help" butcher a cow or a pig. Brandy had not been born into the community, but she had moved into the abandoned third House eight years ago and so far no one—not even Dan Aucheron—had found a reason to throw her out. She was a huge, heavy woman given to talking to herself aloud and prowling the roads for hours in search of who knew what. But she had undeniable skill—or good luck—as a farmer. Her marijuana patch more than made up for her eccentricities. And she was Arrowsmith's only recent "convert."

"What did she say?" Neil wanted to know.

"Oh, she went on and on," Elizabeth said. "It was something about smoke coming from the yard."

"From the *Quiller* place?" Cissy Funderburk stirred at the head of the table. "I thought that place went completely to weed forty years ago."

"It did," Elizabeth said, "but Barbara says she was up near Willow Ridge right about sunset and saw smoke—you know how that place sits right down in that gully—and it couldn't have come from anywhere else."

Neil spoke up between bites. "That's funny. I was just over to New House talking to Cory about an hour ago and he said something like that, too."

"He saw smoke?" Jeremy said.

"He saw a campfire. He was coming back from hunting and I guess it was dark enough—"

"Neil, the only way you could see a fire in that farmyard is to be *in* the yard. What kind of hunting would he be doing there? Was anyone else with him?" Cory was several years younger than Neil and Jeremy and considered to be a bit of a layabout.

Ben said to Jeremy, "Why not let him tell it before you go jumping all over him?"

"Ben—" Elizabeth said.

Jeremy felt his face go red. He considered three replies, but did not use them. Better just to shut up.

"Oh hell," Neil said. "I didn't *believe* him. He probably *was* over to Brandy's getting high. I only brought it up because Brandy saw something, too. I mean, Cory told me he thought it was Brandy's fire anyway."

"Brandy's not in the habit of setting fires and then leaving them," Ben said.

"Who else would it be?" Heather said. "She's the only person who lives anywhere near that farm."

Ben turned to Neil. "Did Cory see anything else? Any signs of people?" Jeremy knew what Ben was thinking: outlaws.

"If he did, he didn't say. I don't suppose he got close enough to tell. He was probably cutting across the ridge from Brandy's and saw some smoke from the distance, like she did."

"I wonder if he's told Dan," Ben said quietly, with a glance at Cissy. "Somebody ought to take a look, just in case."

"Somebody *should* tell Dan," Cissy repeated. She was Dan's watchdog at Hill House. The joke was that she knew more about what Dan would think than Dan would.

Ben seemed worried now, and it was justified. Jeremy hoped that the mysterious campfire was indeed Brandy Kramer's—or better yet, a figment of Cory's chemically enhanced imagination. In its present weakened condition, the community would have a hard time surviving a second outlaw attack.

The first attackers, five years ago, had been well equipped, to the point where they were driving a more recent model troop carrier than the local CSA detachment.

Five years ago there were still half a dozen people living at Sun House. Only two were home when the outlaws appeared from the south, up from the flatlands in the center of the state, fresh, it was later learned, from raids on the highway between Dubuque and Waterloo. No one in Arrowsmith, of course, had any warning that there was a band in the neighborhood—another benefit of Dan's isolationism. The whole Texan Army could have been driving through the hills and no one in Arrowsmith would have known. They might never have known about that first bunch if Thea Zappa and Rhiannon Sharps hadn't set fire to Sun House as a desperate signal. The fire drew the attention of Ed Potratz, who, from the relative safety of Willow Ridge, saw the outlaw vehicles and horses and ran yelling to Hill House.

The first scouts, Ben included, found the outlaws camped right in the middle of the huge garden that Rhiannon had worked so hard for so long to grow. The raiders must have thought they had stumbled upon some lesbian haven—women alone—because they only posted a single guard while the others enjoyed themselves.

Heard in the retold version, Ben killed that guard with a shovel and the rest of the Arrowsmith vigilantes drove off the surviving outlaws with ease. But Jeremy had heard the story straight from Ben and knew better:

They had waited until dark, not out of any shrewd sense of strategy, but because they had to send back to New House for a pair of old rifles. When those arrived Ben took one and, slipping up to the house, at close range shot the guard in the back. He told Jeremy later he'd gotten that close because he was afraid the gun wouldn't fire; in that case he planned to club the outlaw to death.

The noise brought the rest of the outlaws out of the house, where Ben and the others were waiting with their two rifles and their bows, axes, and shovels. Their first ragged volley cut down a pair of outlaws, but the survivors—ten or more—managed to reach the horses and the troop carrier. Some terrible weapon mounted on the carrier cut Ed Potratz in half and chewed up Crystal Aucheron, too. Ben and the rest simply ran. Left behind, Crystal died. There was a lot of trouble about that later. The outlaw truck, escorted by men on horseback, wounded four more members of the community before rumbling off into the night.

So Ben's company had killed one outlaw and wounded a pair, one of whom crawled into the barn and was later found. At dawn the next day they hanged him from a tree near Hill House and threw his body into the old quarry. Then they buried Ed Potratz and Crystal Aucheron in the fields. They also buried Thea Zappa, who hadn't been durable enough for the outlaws' evening of sport. A month later they also buried Rhiannon Sharps.

Even so, they were lucky. If the outlaws had not withdrawn, had they stood their ground, the community might have died five years ago.

"I'll go down to the House and talk to Dan first thing in the morning," Ben told Cissy. "Maybe we—"

The two lights in Hill House flickered, then went out. Around the table several people started talking at once. "Get the candles!" Elizabeth ordered.

"Where are you going?" Heather whispered. Jeremy was getting up from the bench. *"Jeremy!"*

But he was already out the door. He didn't bother to put on a coat.

The autumn night was clear, cold, and windy, with the stars shining brightly overhead. Stumbling across the lumpy field toward the base of the tower, he could have cared less.

You son of a bitch, he thought.

People were calling his name from the House. He didn't feel like answering.

Now, there were five basic parts to his power system: rotor, generator, converter, lights, and wind. If any one element was missing, the whole thing failed. He knew that the lights worked, so he could forget them. The lights wouldn't have gone on in the first place if the generator didn't work, so that wasn't the problem. The wind was blowing . . . It had to be the generator, or the rotor itself.

He stared up into the darkness, looking at the tip of the tower. He could see that the rotor was still there, and still in one piece.

But it wasn't turning.

That meant the generator was broken. Frozen, maybe. Damn. He slammed his fist into the nearest upright. He wanted to cry. A generator failure was simply beyond his ability to fix.

Suddenly there were warm hands around his stomach and a face in the nape of his neck. He didn't move. "You shouldn't have come out here," he said.

"Neither should you," Heather said. "Not without a coat. Besides, I'm pregnant, not sick."

He turned and took her in his arms. "I'm not going to be able to fix it."

"I'm sorry, Jeremy, really." She tried to smile. "But life goes on. We've lived for a long time without electricity . . ."

He pushed her away. "It's *more* than that, Heather!" He knew he was frightening her but he couldn't stop. "Don't you understand that? Doesn't anybody?" Some of the others had come out of the House and stood behind her. Elizabeth, Ben, and, carrying Jeremy's coat, Neil.

"Jeremy, maybe we could get some parts in town . . ." That was Elizabeth.

"You mean we could all work on it together?" He couldn't hide the bitterness in his voice. He started to walk away, hearing Ben's low, "Let him be for a while," which only made him angrier. *One of his moods, you know. Jeremy always was a hot-headed kid.* Yeah, he was being moody when he couldn't get that old tractor to work. Just being a little hot-headed when he tried to understand what the words in their old medical books meant. Right now he wanted to keep walking until he reached West Union, or one of the agrifactories. He wanted to forget about Heather and the child and the whole idea of a neat little life in Arrowsmith. They were blind and doomed, all of them.

Neil caught up with him at the road. He held out his coat and said, "Better take this." Jeremy put it on. He had started to get cold. "Hey," Neil said, "why don't we go over to Brandy's?"

"Sounds like a good idea," Jeremy said. And they started up the road.

CHAPTER 7

Outlaw Territory, Wednesday Morning

"What do you see?" Rob Prescott asked.

He lay on a bed of needles beneath a young pine tree. A hundred yards downriver and maybe ten yards below him sat the Slougham Road bridge, which crossed the Turkey River east of West Union. Right now Prescott's clear view was dominated by Stagger's muddy boots. The younger man sprawled in front of him on the slope, peering over the crest toward the bridge.

"Looks deader than Dubuque on a Sunday night," Stagger said.

Prescott took that to mean it was clear. Sometimes it was hard telling with Stagger. He was just some kid they'd caught stealing from one of their tents the time they'd laid over in Manchester. Instead of cutting his throat they'd recruited him. Prescott occasionally wondered if they'd made the right decision. Stagger was an incurable sneak and not even close to reliable, but he was fast as the devil, quick with a knife, and had the best eyesight in the bunch.

Prescott slipped down to the road, sweeping the needles from his chest and beard. They'd been on the move since dawn, maybe an hour ago now, having slept in their vehicles the night before. Once across the Turkey they would find good roads—meaning clear roads —all the way to the Minnesota line. Then it would be time to relax, though you could never really relax when you made your living raiding convoys.

"Let's get a move on," he told the others, climbing behind the wheel of his jeep. He usually went second in the outlaw train, right behind their pride and joy, a '32 Ford carrier with official CSA markings, right in front of their cargo wagon and the second jeep. Prescott formerly drove point, but his windshield had once stopped a bullet aimed directly at his face and now he preferred to remain in the shadow of the battlewagon. "Check your gauges, girls. Go potty. We won't be stopping till Harmony." That would be noon at the latest.

Stagger jumped into the seat beside him. Prescott generally did his own driving, not out of necessity, but simply because he enjoyed it. Looking back, it was one of the attractions of this business.

In front of them the carrier started up, belching a smelly cloud of exhaust. "You think that pile of junk is even going to make it to the line?" Stagger said.

"It'll have to. We don't have room in the back seat for what it's carrying."

What was in the carrier, and in the wagon, was plunder from ten days of raids on the Omaha–Des Moines–Davenport route, Highway 80. Enough goodies to bring a smile to the faces of their fences from the People's Republic, and to carry all of them through the winter. Right now a second train was moving toward the Harmony rendezvous through New Hampton, thirty miles the other side of West Union. It went against company rules, splitting up like that, but you had to know the peculiarities of the CSA garrisons nearby. West Union's two dozen troopers were responsible for something like four hundred square miles, the whole northeast sector of the state. They had a history of going after any and all reported outlaw trains rather than concentrating on one at a time. A single train wouldn't have much chance against a troop of CSA armored cav, but put them up against a unit half that size, or a third . . . well, that was the principle by which they lived.

Prescott gunned the jeep. Behind him the wagon creaked into motion, its driver whipping the team, the pair of shotguns holding on for dear life. Canfield brought up the rear in their second jeep, the one that carried all their comm gear: radios, CB, GPS, fuzzbusters.

Stagger was singing to himself. "Knock it off," Prescott snapped. Stagger liked to annoy people, as if he just wanted to make sure you knew he was around. Normally Prescott would let him yammer, but it was too nice a morning for that. A peaceful morning, good for a long run to the state line.

His dash CB squawked. He thumbed the speaker. "Yeah."

"I picked up something while you and Stagger were up on the ridge," Canfield said. "Thought you might be interested."

Up ahead the carrier was making the final turn onto the bridge. "Shoot."

"There was an all-points on channel fifty," Canfield said. Channel fifty was a military band. Prescott and his outlaws wouldn't normally have access to it, but they had captured a CSA receiver intact during the raid on Elk Run Heights. "Sounds like the whole Third Division's going on alert."

"Somebody start a war?" The Third Division meant over a thousand soldiers. "What's that got to do with us?"

"I don't know," Canfield said. "But there'll be bluejackets crawling out of the woodwork."

"Thanks." Prescott downshifted to take the little rise leading up to the bridge. The carrier, going slowly, as usual, was halfway across. Prescott stayed in low gear, almost idling, to give the bigger vehicle time to reach the other shore, fifty yards away. He turned toward Stagger—

"Incoming!" Stagger screamed, tearing his rifle off the rack.

Downriver, just over the treetops, came a CSA helicopter. It was heading right for them.

The carrier reached the far shore just as the chopper's guns stitched the bridge, sending pebbles and chunks of masonry into the air.

Prescott jammed the jeep into reverse, but he wasn't getting off the bridge until the wagon behind him could clear the way.

Stagger leaped out of the jeep, blasting away at the chopper as it finished its first pass and made a tight climb and turn not far upriver. It was coming back for another crack at them.

"Stagger! Get your ass back in here!" Prescott shouted, but there was no talking to Stagger at a time like this.

Here we go again, Prescott thought. The chopper was a Toyota Banshee, ten years old at least, more suited to police work than combat, carrying a heavy machine gun, maybe two, but not much more. It was really a scout ship.

A scout could kill you just as dead . . .

He popped the clutch as the chopper's guns swung his way and the jeep lurched forward suddenly, avoiding a good chewing. Whoever was up there was good.

Whump! A fireball bloomed on the bank where the carrier waited. A bomb? Prescott blinked to get rid of the afterimage, suddenly aware of all the noise around him. Several autorifles chattered away. There were shouts and screams.

Enough of this. Prescott whipped the jeep in a tight Y-turn and tore back to the relative safety of the south bank. The wagon was finally out of the way.

He passed Stagger, who was crouched behind the retaining wall, peppering the oncoming chopper with true manic intensity. Prescott was too busy driving to look, but he thought he heard a telltale twang! as the Banshee swooped overhead on its third pass. That'd get the bastards' attention! He rolled off the bridge into the trees and almost rammed a tree.

On the far shore the carrier burned. "Johnston!" Prescott shouted. There was no sign of the driver.

Possibly wounded now, the Banshee broke off the battle and disappeared upriver, to the west. It was quiet on the river again, except for the crackling fire and a distant moaning. Prescott got out of the jeep and checked with Rickie, the wagon driver, and his two shotgunrs. All of them were okay. Stagger was still on the bridge, rifle ready, daring the Banshee to return.

Canfield ran up. "I was listening in. They reported our location, said they've got us moving north toward Gunder and Postville."

"They'll probably try to cut us off there, then," Prescott said tiredly. He rubbed his eyes. Stone chips had irritated them. "Well, there isn't a hell of a lot we get from walking into another ambush. We'll have to lay low for a few days, try to sneak over the line when it's cooled off around here."

Canfield nodded, looking toward the north shore and the fire.

Prescott grabbed the first-aid kit from the jeep, and followed Rickie and the others across the bridge.

Jeremy knew he was in trouble the moment he awoke. It wasn't the first-class headache from last night's close encounter with

Brandy's moonshine that told him so, either. It was the light in the eastern sky.

He and Neil had not gone back to Hill House.

With some effort he sat up and groaned, waking Neil, who lay across the loft. "Go back to bed," Neil croaked.

Jeremy blinked. The view from the loft of the Sun House barn was hardly inspiring. Several panes of glass were missing and had been replaced with wood. Even so, Jeremy could tell that the sun was well up, though the cloudy sky made it impossible to know how long. "Can't," he told Neil. "I've got barn duty today."

"It'll keep till this afternoon."

"Cissy and Dan won't, though."

Neil rolled over and peered at Jeremy. His eyes barely opened. "Let them scream. What difference does it make, anyway? Isn't that what you're always saying?"

"I guess." In his present condition Jeremy didn't feel much like arguing. "Are you coming, too?" he asked as he put on his pants.

"Nope." Neil burrowed back into his blankets. "They'll have to drag me away. Besides, I'm off today."

"Then you don't have worry about them coming to drag you away. I do." Jeremy started for the door. "I wonder where Brandy is."

"Take a look at this place and tell me how much time she spends here."

Jeremy had to concede the point. Sun House had seen its best days. Aside from the broken windows, the furnishings had rotted or disappeared completely, the roof leaked, and ancient balls of dust and dirt grazed freely. Brandy had a lean-to on the outside of the building and it was clear that that was her shelter. She spent most of her time up on Willow Ridge with her beloved still, or off in the woods with her pot.

"I don't suppose I'm going to find anything to drink in here," Jeremy said.

"How about some of Brandy's best?"

Jeremy's stomach vetoed that idea. "No way. I'll see you tonight, then."

"Yeah. Or tomorrow."

Sun House was nestled in a valley four miles due north of Hill and New Houses, which were the original dwellings of the Arrowsmith community. Jeremy's most direct route home was due south. Trouble was, the terrain between the two points was wooded, cut by several tiny creeks that emptied into the Turkey, and roughened by a number of hills that two miles to the west became Willow Ridge. The old roads were no help, either, running as they did at an angle across his path of travel. Jeremy had to walk around three sides of a square to reach Hill House.

But he had barely let Sun House out of sight when he realized that a short detour would bring him close to the Quiller place. It would mean a cross-country hike, but at this time of year the undergrowth was dead and beaten down, especially if you stuck to the ridge tops. He left the road and trudged up a hill.

The sun peeked through the clouds at last, adding some needed brightness to the scene. Wisps of fog were still visible in valleys still shadowed from the sun. Off to the south a pair of smoke columns could be seen: the Houses. Not far below the ridge crest a brook slapped noisily as it tumbled toward the Turkey. Jeremy squinted. Where was that old farmhouse, anyway?

He hoped to see smoke or another sign to the west, but found nothing, so he kept moving along the crest.

When Arrowsmith was founded it consisted of just the two Houses and their parcels of land. The rest of the farms in the area belonged to various agribusinesses or private owners until the years of the Collapse, when marginal plots like the Quiller farm were abandoned one by one. When the last of the Quillers died or went broke—no one seemed to remember exactly what the story was—what was left of the county government had come to attach it. But before the farm could be auctioned the wars broke out and there were no takers. So the Quiller family's proud spread was, in effect, given over to squatters, who quickly found that the almost inaccessible location and rocky ground made it a poor choice for unmechanized farming. They left it alone, as did the people of Arrowsmith, by now settled comfortably in their three Houses.

And there it was, below and to his left, hidden in a grove of oaks.

Dawn was the best time of day to be brave, especially if you were a bit hung over. Jeremy took a deep breath and started down the hill.

At the bottom he found an ancient dirt road barely wide enough to let a wagon pass. Nevertheless, the road took up most of the flat bottomland in the hollow. No wonder people left the Quiller farm alone. Here he was, not a hundred yards from the entrance, and there wasn't a sign of it. He hoped he wouldn't have to fight his way in . . . there were better ways to spend a morning.

Then he saw tracks in the road.

For a moment he was grateful for his weakened condition and the fact that it was still early in the day. Had he been capable of demonstrating great excitement he would be tearing back up the hill, because this road was torn by wagon ruts, hoofprints, and truck tires. The truck markings could have belonged to CSA patrols, but Jeremy had never heard of a combined truck-and-horse-drawn-wagon unit.

Outlaws had passed through the hollow.

He forced himself to keep walking. He had come down from the hill in a sunny spot and the ruts had softened in the morning thaw. He needed to see them in the shade to know how long ago they were made.

He shivered as the sun disappeared behind the hill, but knew it wasn't the cold that did that. His jacket was quite warm.

He scuffed his boot in the fat tire tracks. They seemed frozen. He spotted a trail of horse apples. They looked pretty cold, too.

He relaxed and started walking again, knowing that the outlaws were at least half a day away. That would put them far past the Quiller place and, he hoped, on the road to Minnesota.

Then branches snapped ahead of him and he thought he would fill his pants. Stupidly he crouched, as if hoping for some magic invisibility . . . or maybe a quick death.

Someone was pushing through the growth along the road.

Jeremy had to make a choice. He had the advantage of a clear field behind him while the source of his unease was still some distance from the road. If he turned tail now he would have a good chance to get away clean. He was a fast runner and this was his home ground. Or he could rely on his earlier judgment. A man stupid enough to misread simple tracks was as good as dead, anyway. What would Ben do in a situation like this?

Jeremy headed toward the noise.

The sounds kept coming closer and getting louder. There was the whipping and cracking of branches being pushed aside, the thudding of heavy boots against hard earth, slipping and sliding followed by inaudible oaths. In these shadows Jeremy's visibility was limited to a few feet. To make matters worse, the ground sloped sharply up from the road, effectively blocking his view.

Suddenly, not ten feet away, a person dropped to the road, falling on his behind. The hiker said something unpleasant, then saw Jeremy for the first time. "Oh my God."

It was the woman he'd seen in West Union. The woman with the tricar and the alien in the back seat.

CHAPTER 8

Austin, Great Texas,
Wednesday Morning

"Here's the report from the Governor's party, Chief."

Captain Tim Strauss, Great Texas Department of Public Safety—also known as the Texas Rangers—tapped the display key on his desk comsole. The viewscreen lit up with the unhappy news. "Is this all we have, Mr. Levin?"

"Right now," his assistant replied. "The Governor may be calling shortly. That's the message, anyway."

"Thank you." Strauss took out a cigarette and tapped it on the screen before lighting it. He took a drag, then sat back, swiveling his chair. From his corner office in the newest government office building (as opposed to the merely new and newer ones) he had a clear view of the "gargoyles" adorning the Driskill Hotel across San Jacinto Street. Those faces had seen the entire interregnum between the First Texas Republic and the Second, or so the story went. No doubt they would see the Third. Strauss had his doubts.

He was full of doubts these days.

The report was too sketchy to be much more than an annoyance. Dr. Lisa Marquez, Special Assistant (Science and Technology) to the Governor of Great Texas, was missing. Missing with her was a very expensive and specially modified Oberheim Hurricane, said vehicle last seen exiting Chicago municipal airspace at an illegal high rate of speed. Subsequent sightings of the vehicle on outstate radars were inconsistent with known performance parameters and not confirmed. What could be confirmed was that the Hurricane and the assistant were not where they were supposed to be. End of report.

And this had taken almost two days? What were they thinking of up in Chicago?

It might have remained a complicated but routine problem, since it was not unknown for civil servants to go astray, but for the joker in this particular deck. Also missing was a member of the Hocq mission, which had been touring the People's Republic under a quadrilateral "trade" agreement between Great Texas, Chicago, California, and the extraterrestrials' actual hosts, the Afro-Soviet Union. Strauss was grateful for one thing: this had happened in Chicago, not in Dallas. The Africans could hardly accuse their own allies of revisionist-imperialist hooliganism.

There was a second page to the report and Strauss scrolled to it. His agent in place, under diplomatic cover, was a young man named Shapiro, the perfect choice when it came to dealings with the Chicagoans . . . but not, perhaps, best suited to the new situation. Shapiro had actually appended an action memorandum straight out of the civil service manual to his report:

CATEGORY ONE: [Most likely] Kidnapping
   (Political)
CATEGORY TWO: Kidnapping (Criminal)
CATEGORY THREE: Defection

Strauss sighed. He honestly didn't give a good goddamn about Doug Shapiro's evaluation; he wanted the facts. All the report told him was that the pool security check of the room at eleven-thirty CST Sunday showed that one of the Hocq, Harrek by name, was missing from his suite at the Hilton. A further routine check of the human members of the mission made it apparent that Dr. Marquez was also missing, as was one of the Hurricanes specially modified to serve as Hocq transport. Signs of struggle? Strauss had to assume not, since there was no mention of any. Interviews with hotel staff? Also missing. Even the routine correlation between vehicle disappearances and Chicago traffic reports was not performed until Monday morning, by which time a Hurricane could have reached the Cleveland spill or the Dakota Nation.

This was no good. Strauss couldn't really blame Shapiro, since a defection of this magnitude was out of his league. He blamed the so-

called pool security people—Africans and Russians, in particular—
who were so busy spying on their comrades that they forgot that
intelligent, bull-headed individuals like the Hocq would do unpredictable things . . .

"Captain?" It was Levin on the intercom. "The Governor is calling."

"Great." He snuffed the cigarette and ran a hand over his bald
spot. "Put her through."

He needn't have worried about his appearance; the call was audio
only, encrypted and patched through Texatcom rather than through
the archaic People's Republic system. "Have you seen Shapiro's report, Tim?" Governor Ruthven said. She sounded unusually tired.

"I just finished it."

"As you can imagine, we've got a real mess on our hands. I suppose you heard about the California cancellation—" No he had not.
Damn Shapiro anyway! "—on top of this . . . unfortunate occur-
rence. Boroz, their senior, had urged us in particular . . . by that I
mean Texas . . . to do what we can to recover their missing person.
She indicated to me her unhappiness with the Union's security appa-
ratus and with the local investigation, and I can't say that I blame
her.

"Naturally," the Governor went on, "being able to get Marquez
and the alien back would not only erase this blot from our record—
though Boroz isn't blaming Texas yet; she says her brother is crazy—
but it might just be the move that puts us in good with the Hocq, and
you know what that means."

"I understand, Governor." He sure did. The Hocq, it seemed,
were finally ready to come across with the Genesis materials. Everyone wanted them but only one country would get them. "Uh, Governor, had you talked to Marquez at all?"

"Do you mean, did I detect anything that would lead me to suspect she might be up to something? No, but I haven't exchanged
more than two words with her since we met the mission in Miami.
She was harassed, of course, but Genesis is her baby, and besides,
you know Lisa."

"Indeed I do," Strauss said, by reflex suppressing a smile.

"I think you'd be a good choice, then."

"Choice for what, Governor?" He didn't like the sound of that at all.

"We want someone to take charge of the investigation. You know Marquez, the Californians, Russians and Africans all feel it's a Texas problem, let Texas fix it, and I don't know who else I'd trust to deal with the Central States."

"Central States?"

"Oh, I'm sorry. They've tracked the missing car to Iowa. Doug Shapiro is on his way there now and says he can pick you up tonight in . . . what is this name? Dubuque. I have to go on to Minneapolis with the mission."

"That sounds fine, Governor. I'll leave as soon as I can."

They broke the connection. Dubuque, Strauss thought with disdain. The Central States. He felt as tired as Ruthven sounded. "Mr. Levin?"

"Yes, Chief?"

"It appears that I need to reach Dubuque, Iowa, sometime tonight. I think that's somewhere near Des Moines, but I was never any good at geography. Can you make arrangements? There must be a wagon train or a riverboat heading north."

Levin laughed. "I'll try."

"Please do. I'm going to run home and pack."

He leaned back in his chair and closed his eyes. A fugitive Hocq and Lisa Marquez . . . both of them on the loose in the Central States. Strauss could think of a less complicated assignment.

An assassination, for instance.

"I don't believe it," Lisa told Jeremy, as they emerged from the woods into the Quiller farmyard. They had made wary introductions and now, half a mile later, were old friends. "I feel so stupid. I might have wandered around for a week if you hadn't found me."

"Oh, eventually you'd have found your way," Jeremy said.

"Don't be too sure of that. I've got a Ph.D. in ineptitude and it shows whenever I get too far from pavement and artificial light." She noticed him staring at the Hurricane, which was parked nearby. "Hey, at least I can offer you some coffee. Come on."

He followed, though not without some hesitation. The Quiller place was haunted, people said. So far he had seen nothing to dispute that.

"Wait here, Jeremy. I'll be back in a second." Lisa disappeared behind the Hurricane. When she returned she was looking nervously over her shoulder toward an orange tent planted next to the ruined farmhouse. Jeremy hadn't noticed it until now.

"Is something wrong?"

"No, no," she said, momentarily distracted. She bent to stir at a cold fire.

Jeremy's eyes kept returning to the tricar. It looked somewhat less distinguished in the morning light, out in the open like this, especially with one of its front fans in pieces. Still—

"Like the car?"

He blushed. Lisa was smiling at him. She stood up, wiping her hands on her pants. "Come on, I'll give you the dollar tour. Coffee'll be a few minutes, anyway."

She walked over to the car with Jeremy hurrying after her. He stood aside as she opened the heavy driver's door, swinging it toward the sky. "Careful," she said. "Now you can go inside."

Jeremy required no further encouragement. The seat was more comfortable than his bed at Hill House. Had he not been so excited he would have taken a nap.

Lisa got in on the passenger side. "Okay, lesson time. I'm going to assume, just for the sake of argument, that you've never been inside one of these babies before." She laughed and so did Jeremy. "Anyway, this is the dashboard or instrument panel, depending on whether you're technically minded or not. You can see we've got air and ground speed indicators, engine readouts, fuel gauges, the works. Over there's the gyro display to show you whether or not your fans are in balance. Here, of course, is the guidance computer . . ."

It was already too much for Jeremy. The words simply ran together in his head. "Actually," Lisa said gently, "once you get the car started"—she nodded toward the ignition key—"almost everything is automatic. The tiller controls your direction. Point it where you want to go and that's it." Jeremy had his hands on the tiller. Gingerly, he moved it. "This is the throttle," Lisa continued. "In this position there's no power, up here you have a lot of power. Simple, isn't it?"

"Yeah." But he felt stupider than he'd ever felt in his life. Even so, he would have given a month's meals for a ride.

Lisa opened a panel in the dash and began fiddling with it. "And now it's your turn to answer a few of *my* questions."

"I can't believe there's anything I could tell you."

"Trust me. Look, Jeremy, I'm a stranger here, and, as you can see, I'm stuck. All I know about this area is what I learned in the fifth grade. Now, you've told me that when we first met in West Union that it was the first time you'd ever been to town. So where do you live?"

There was something in her voice that made him want to help. "A couple of miles south of that ridge."

"Alone or with family?" Lisa continued to touch buttons on the dash. The result was a series of bleeps and squawks interspersed with voices.

"Family . . . I guess."

Lisa turned to him. "You guess. Okay. How many?"

"Close to fifty."

"Fifty? In a single family?"

"Well, it's not really a single family," he insisted. "It's a community—"

"A commune! Okay, I understand that. Like the Amish or Hook-and-Eye-Dutch? Damn!" She stabbed furiously at the panel. "What's it all about?"

"What do you mean?"

"What's the group? Are you Moonies, Scientologists, Pilgrims, Aryan Knights? I thought that's what communes were all about."

"I—"

"Wait a second." She held up her hand, saving Jeremy from a confusing answer. A voice came out of the dashboard. "—APB, priority two. Subject is female, description to follow, piloting a twenty-twenty-nine Oberheim Hurricane, Texas plates, last seen exiting Chicago airspace Sunday evening. She's believed to be traveling on the surface in an area north of a line connecting Dubuque and Waterloo and south of the Minnesota border. Caution is advised—she may be

armed and is certainly dangerous. In addition, she is accompanied by
—" Lisa cut off the transmission. "They didn't waste any time," she
said softly.

"Red knew you were from Texas."

"Red's a smart guy," she snapped. "We're easy to spot in these
parts. We're the ones with two heads." She sighed. "I'm sorry. I'm
not angry at you."

"That's all right."

"Can you tell me one thing? Did you and Red take a look inside
the car?"

"Yeah. Did we get you in trouble?"

She laughed. "I got in quite enough trouble on my own, thank
you. No, I just need to know who has seen me." With a faraway look
in her eyes, Lisa opened her door and got out. Jeremy took that as a
suggestion that he do likewise. With some difficulty he managed to
find the proper handle and push the door open.

"Look," Lisa told him, "you were very kind to walk me home, but
you should probably be going. It's going to get very crowded around
here and you don't want to get in the middle of it."

She looked tired and frail. Jeremy found himself saying, "Let me
help."

That won him a smile. "You don't know how I'd love to take you
up on that, Jeremy. But there are too many powerful forces at work
here. You could get chewed up—" She paused, looking over Jeremy's
shoulder. "Harrek!"

Jeremy whirled too quickly. Before him, encased in a silver and
white suit, stood a creature seven feet tall with four snaky arms.

That was all he saw.

"Feeling better now?"

Jeremy was in the cruiser again, in the driver's seat, a damp cloth
on his head. His hangover was back, reinforced. "I think so," he
said, looking up at Lisa, who leaned in through the open door. Beyond her stood the creature, as motionless as a tree on a winter day.

Jeremy would not allow himself to look away. He convinced himself that the creature's appearance, though strange, didn't bother
him. "Did I faint?" he asked.

"Not quite," Lisa said. "What you did was wang your head on the door." She pointed to the edge of the open door. "Right about there. I bet that hurt."

"It still does." He started to get up.

"Take it easy, Jeremy."

That struck him as a useful suggestion. "So that's a Hocq."

"Yep. And it's time you two were formally introduced." She moved aside, giving Jeremy his first unobstructed view of the creature. He had gotten used to the unnatural height and skinniness of the Hocq, and to the strange protective garment. It was tougher to accept the two sets of arms, one short pair up around the creature's neck, one longer, multijointed pair that, of all things, seemed to be attached somewhere around the knees, though the "hands" rode at waist level.

Then there was the face. Even though it was covered with a clear, bubblelike helmet, it seemed too large, wrong, somehow. The closest thing to it in looks was a dog's face, since the mouth—which didn't contain teeth—was wider than a human's and constantly open. A three-pronged tongue was also plainly evident.

The creature was quick to react when Lisa spoke to him. He started to move, making a sound like a train of wagons going over a bumpy road, wobbling with an uncertain, up-and-down gait that reminded Jeremy of a man who was completely drunk. The legs wobbled at the knees as the creature's big flat feet rose and fell. There was motion from the lower pair of arms as well, which fluttered like the wings of a bird one moment and, in the next, actually brushed the ground ahead of the feet, tossing aside good-sized rocks and pulling up dead grass with amazing quickness.

Jeremy got out of the car. He didn't want to face this lying down.

"Harrek al-Khittim, I'd like you to meet Jeremy Clayton."

The Hocq bent forward, wrapping its upper—lesser—arms around Jeremy's head. The touch was brief and no worse than having a human put gloved hands on your ears. At the same time a voice spoke from a box on the creature's chest. "I'm pleased to meet you, Jeremy. I've seen you before."

Jeremy was a bit disappointed. The creature sounded more human than alien. "We saw each other in West Union."

"Before you two start chatting about the weather," Lisa said, "you may want to know that Harrek noted some kind of disturbance this morning, not far from here."

"I didn't hear anything," Jeremy said.

"When he's in the suit Harrek has augmented sensory capabilities. He hears better than we do."

"Well, then what kind of disturbance did he sense?"

Harrek said, "Several humans, animals, and machines in armed conflict. This occurred shortly after local sunrise in that direction." One of the Hocq's lower, greater arms stretched toward the northwest, roughly in the direction of West Union. "I wished to investigate but was unable to reach the location."

Jeremy considered it. "Sometimes there are CSA troops out on maneuvers." At least, that was what he'd learned on Monday. He didn't want to appear ignorant. Then he had a horrible thought: the tracks!

"Whatever it was, it woke me up, too," Lisa said. "And to Harrek's sensors it must have sounded like World War Four."

"It could be outlaws," Jeremy said.

Her eyes narrowed. "What makes you say that?"

"You asked me what group I lived with. We don't have a name. We aren't part of any movement. We reject that. But there are people around who are."

"Aryan Knights."

Jeremy nodded. "Either them or the Christian Marauders." The outlaw bands dated back to the 1980s. At first they were farmers who lost their farms and blamed either the federal government or the big banks or the Jews—usually all three—and took to the woods. The collapse had convinced them they were right, and made them stronger.

Lisa looked sick. "How many and how much trouble are they?"

"There won't be more than a dozen," Jeremy said, repeating information he'd heard for years, that the outlaws traveled in small groups. "But they'll be armed."

"And here I sit with a broken car."

Jeremy glanced at the surrounding hills. It had to be past mid-morning, but it was hard to tell, since the sky was almost a uniform gray. He shivered. "Maybe you better move that tent out of sight," he told Lisa. "I'll help. I'll have to go home for a while, but I'll come back."

Lisa nodded. "Thanks."

He would tell Ben about the outlaw tracks. He would not tell him about Lisa and Harrek. He was going to be in enough trouble.

CHAPTER 9

Outlaw Territory, Wednesday Afternoon

The retreat from the bridge took all day. They lost one precious hour burying the dead shotgun and trying to salvage what they could from the burning carrier. Its driver, Johnston, had been thrown by the explosion and now lay in the back of the wagon, probably bleeding to death.

It was a slow retreat because of their well-rehearsed emergency tactics, which were designed to keep them safe from another ambush, and from overhead detection. The principle was to move quickly from one place of cover to another, then wait, and move again. Cover was easy to find in this terrain. The hills that loomed over twisting Slougham Road were dense with trees and brush. It was the protective cover, however, that also kept them crawling. They had a pair of shotguns fanned out ahead of the column, on foot, one man keeping to the road, the other—Stagger—moving parallel to the road on higher ground. Both men carried short-range Ku-band radios, which were essential for secure communications but annoying because they limited the column to strictly line-of-sight contact. It was pretty tricky to maintain line-of-sight in these hills, but there was no other choice.

"Rob?" It was Stagger on the com.

"Yeah."

"I'm looking down at the Slougham-Arrowsmith crossroads. If you're thinking of going east on Arrowsmith, tell me now, because it's going to be a bitch and a half getting over to the other side."

"Wait one." Prescott got out of his jeep and walked toward the rear of the column, passing the wagon team with its three heavy-breathing, wet-sided horses. They were drawing an extra-heavy load now and wouldn't go much farther without rest.

Canfield brought up the rear in his mobile listening post. "What's playing?" Prescott asked.

"Same old song," Canfield said. "From what I can tell, they really are deploying the Third—a good part of it, anyway."

"Jesus H. Christ." Prescott felt sick. It was bad enough losing a man and half their stash to a single chopper. You could consider that exceptionally high overhead if you wanted. But there was no doing business with a whole division on the roads. The only thing you could do then was hide out.

"There's something funny about this, though," Canfield added. "I don't think it's *us* they're after."

"Well, who else would they be looking for? The Texan Army?"

Canfield ignored the sarcasm. "They aren't deploying for combat and they aren't staking out our routes. They're setting up for road-block work, interdiction, over a very large area, something like three hundred square miles."

"Why would they do that? All the chopper had to do was call in and they'd have us pinned within ten miles or so."

"That's what I mean. It doesn't make sense." Canfield shook his head. "One other thing. They've got some code name for this operation. They keep talking about 'hawks.' "

Prescott began to notice a chill in the air. The wind was rising and the sky was growing darker. "Hawks?"

"Yeah. All I know for sure is that there's one hell of a big mobilization on. Those blue boys will have to get their fat asses out of bed and onto the roads." He grinned. "They won't be happy."

"The line forms to the right." Prescott knew that "hawk" meant Hocq. He couldn't imagine what an alien would be doing out here, and didn't want to know. He only hoped the soldiers would find him and leave Prescott alone. He wanted to go home. "I'd hate to have to hide out around here for long."

"It looks like a pretty good place to me," Canfield said.

"Yeah, but once we get a few miles east of here we run into a commune. A few years ago we made a run through here going south

—I was with the other train, but Stagger was in the one that came this way. They had a real fight on their hands, let me tell you. Couple of guys got killed."

"No fooling? Usually these dirt farmers are happy to see us."

"These aren't dirt farmers. They're *real* private types. To tell you the truth, I've been a little nervous since we got up here last night."

Canfield smiled toothlessly. "Well, we don't have much choice, do we?"

"That's for sure." Prescott slapped the hood of the comm jeep. "Let's get bunkered in before it snows."

When he got back to his jeep the sky was noticeably darker, and not from the setting sun. There were clouds rolling down from Minnesota. "Stagger?"

It was a moment before he got a reply. "Here."

"We'll take Arrowsmith east. Better get across."

"Already there, boss."

Prescott didn't know whether to congratulate him or shoot him. "Get going, then. We need a hideout, now."

"I think I see one."

"We'll be right behind you."

He signaled the train forward, wanting very badly just to gun the jeep and get the hell out of the area. He could almost hear the bluejackets. Digging in for what might be days or even a week . . . that went against all his instincts. Especially when you were in commune territory. There were pockets of them all over the Central States and went right across the board when it came to ideologies and dealings with the real world—he and his men came from one, for that matter. One thing each enclave had in common, though, was a tendency, when it came to dealing with outsiders, to shoot first and ask questions later.

The column reached the Slougham-Arrowsmith junction and Prescott downshifted to take the upgrade. He was grateful again for the little Namibian power plant that burned hydrogen bricks. At least fuel wouldn't be a problem for a few days. By then they would either be out of trouble, or they would be beyond worry.

He slowed down for a rough spot and to let the rest of the train catch up. The laggards were undoubtedly cursing him for breaking his own retreat rules. If there was one thing he had learned in ten years of this life it was that tired, frightened men hated to improvise . . .

He picked up the microphone again. "Hey, Stagger—"

"Not now!" Stagger hissed.

It was hard telling if that was really Stagger, or static. Prescott started to worry again. The rest of the train was still a few minutes behind and he was sitting in an exposed position where the trees had been cleared from one side of the road long ago and had never grown back. On the covered side of the road there was little brush cover, so the presence of trees didn't comfort him, either. He drew his pistol and laid it on the seat within easy reach.

"Okay, Rob." Stagger's voice came out clear. He sounded out of breath. "We can go in. You'll see a dirt road on your right about a hundred yards past this big old billboard—"

"What's wrong with you?"

"Oh"—Stagger giggled—"I had a little discussion with someone . . . about the rent."

"Wait for me."

The wind was growing stronger. Prescott could hear it singing through the trees. He waited until Canfield drove into view, then radioed that he was moving forward and would mark the turn. He spotted the billboard with no trouble—it was a gray frame with just a sole surviving panel and stood not far from the road—and slowed down, looking for Stagger's dirt road.

Stagger stood up from cover. Silently he guided the jeep up the turn and down a long unused driveway.

Prescott parked and got out. "Are we going to be out of sight here?"

"I think so," Stagger said. He was walking with his head down toward a ramshackle house that once upon a time someone had tried to burn down. Abruptly Stagger stopped.

Prescott followed his glance. There in the mud lay a heavy-set young man with a scraggly beard. The boy had wide, staring eyes, and his throat had been cut. Prescott turned to Stagger. "After we get moved in," he said tiredly, "haul him way up the road and dump him. I mean a *long* way.

"Go!"

The end of day or the beginning, it was all the same to Brandy Kramer. Her vision had grown so poor in recent years that a day lacking a bright sun might as well be night. So she kept to schedules of her own making, an arrangement which worked splendidly, as she was the only person affected. Her few head of cattle and three pigs weren't likely to complain. She was left with plenty of time for the work she enjoyed.

She made the long walk back from New House in a foul mood. There had been another unpleasant encounter with Dan Aucheron, who still nursed the fool idea that keeping Brandy away from the main building with its smokehouse and forge would keep anyone in Arrowsmith from using her moonshine or marijuana. In practice, it only meant that Hugh Walton and the others had to walk up to Hill House to see her, which was really very silly, since that trip took two good hours out of a work day while a delivery from Brandy took up just a few minutes. Worse yet, when Brandy delivered the product the recipients tended to save it for hours when they weren't working. When they had to traipse up the Hill . . . well, they tended to roll back down.

She was unable to understand old Dan, anyway. It had taken him ten years to realize that Arrowsmith needed to trade liquor and dope to survive and it would probably take him another ten to figure out that they needed to use the stuff themselves to survive.

Brandy slipped across the spine of Willow Ridge and down its northern slope. Her cows grazed the meadow here, though that would end soon, with the first winter storm. She was ready for it. A little farther around the hill was a shallow cave full of raw hay cut and bound by her own hand. The hay and the animals would keep her warm when the snow fell. Her little pigs were another matter, though, rooting all over the place as they did. They would need to be driven over to Hill House. Tomorrow she could ask Neil to do that for her.

By the time she neared Sun House her annoyance with Dan was completely forgotten, as it always was the farther she got from him.

It was sunset now but she needed no light. Her feet knew the trails better than her clouded eyes did. But as she got close to Sun House she became uneasy. Something in the wind . . . a smell, a voice.

She stopped in her tracks. The smell was horses, the voices were several, none of them familiar. She could make out three or four spots of light.

There were people at Sun House!

Brandy crouched. She had to hide, had to disappear, and not back to the cave, but deep into the woods, where nobody could find her. But where was Neil?

She wrapped her tattered blanket around her shoulders and scrambled up the ridge, into the dark.

Heather was waiting up for Jeremy when he stumbled into Hill House. "It's late," she said.

"I know." That was about all he had the strength to say.

She put her hands on his shoulders and guided him toward a chair. "Sit."

"Is everybody else in bed?"

"Yes. Elizabeth was worried sick about you."

"I guess that means the news has spread." Jeremy had gone straight to work at New House without stopping here. "I told Ben and the rest of them it was only tracks I saw." He had not told Ben and the rest of them about Lisa or Harrek or the "disturbance."

"Well, you know how she gets. I was worried, too." She knelt to unlace his boots. Jeremy had to admit that that was a nice thing for her to do. "Where did they send you today?"

"It seemed like I was everywhere. I did some work for Hugh down in the barn, then had to help store that meat we got from Kelleher's in the smokehouse, then . . . you know, I don't even remember. What did you do today?"

"They had me working in the garden for a while." She blinked. "Which is where you were supposed to be later, as I recall."

"That was the one I couldn't remember."

"Why do you let them do this to you? You know they keep piling it on just to see how long it takes you to say no. They don't really have any right to work you so hard."

He smiled as the second boot dropped with a thump. Then Heather slid into his lap. She was a tiny girl, not much more than an armful, though pregnancy was making it harder for her to move. "I guess I just hate to say no."

"We both know that, don't we?" She kissed him.

Jeremy let his hand drift to her breast. "Getting big, aren't you?"

"That's what happens when you can't say no." She kissed him again, this time slipping her hand inside his shirt. Her touch was warm. After a moment, she said, "I wonder if it's going to be a boy or a girl."

"Does it make any difference?" His words came out sharper than he'd intended.

"Well, maybe it doesn't!" Her disappointment was fleeting. She looked at him sadly. "Poor Jeremy . . . so unhappy."

"So tired."

"Maybe you should spend more nights at home."

"Heather, what's wrong?"

There were tears in her eyes. Jeremy felt them as he brushed her hair back from her face. "I don't know. I guess I'm afraid. I've got this little thing inside me . . . and I don't know just how I'm going to be able to take care of it. I don't know if you're going to be here to help."

"You're hardly alone here, Heather." He coughed, a reflex born of fatigue and reluctance to continue this discussion. "Do you think I'm going somewhere?"

She nodded, and that simple motion filled him with dread, because it struck him with certainty that, yes, he *was* going somewhere . . . anywhere . . . and soon. And that he had been unable to hide it from her. "Look," she said, "I'm a big girl. I *can* take care of myself, and I can take care of a child. I would rather be with you but I'm not going to wither away and die if you run off. I just don't want to see you get hurt."

"This place hurts me, Heather. It's hurting all of us."

Carefully, she stood up. Jeremy was startled to realize how far along she was now: over six months. "It doesn't hurt all of us, Jeremy."

"Suppose I stay, then? We have the baby, we pledge—"

"—If you want. That's not a requirement—"

"—I'd want to. And if we did, there'd be another child before long. Maybe some of the others would have them by then, too, and where are we? More little mouths to feed and less and less to feed them with. We live like *animals*, Heather! There's got to be a better way, for all of us!" He touched her swollen abdomen. "For this one, too."

He put his arms around her, holding her close. None of this was fair and none of it made sense. They had been drawn together in the first place because it was expected of them, because it looked so right, because they had no choice. And he had come to care for her, but she still refused to see their problems, any more than did Dan or Ben or the others. She refused to dream . . .

Yes, Jeremy could spend his life here in Arrowsmith. The Outside world frightened him more than he could admit, especially after today. But he would not surrender to a dead-end life without trying . . . even if it meant that he had to walk away from here without a second glance.

He kissed her, then said, "Why don't you go up to bed? I'm going to get some tea, then I'll be up."

"Okay." She touched a finger to his lips. "Be quiet, though. Everyone else is asleep."

When Heather was gone Jeremy leaned on the counter, looking out the kitchen window, for a long time. They wanted him to work in the garden all day tomorrow . . . well, that would just have to wait. He planned to visit Lisa as soon as he could.

It was a starless, foggy night, and the clouds gave off a frigid glow that made it seem as if nothing moved . . . nothing would ever move.

After a while he went up to bed.

CHAPTER 10

Outlaw Territory, Wednesday Night

His second full day in the wilds of Earth found Harrek somewhat the worse for wear. The constant muscular aches had subsided, thanks to his exercises, and he had recovered some of his former strength, but these ailments had been replaced by new and frightening ones. Now his body seemed swollen, an impression confirmed by pain in the joints of his legs and greater arms, and in the tight fit of his clothing. Worse, he had suffered several spells of illness marked by a discharge that left the cramped tent considerably less comfortable. The odor and attendant mess were enough to overcome his fear of a severe, potentially fatal, Earth infection. He went outside again.

Night had come to Earth, as its pale day star, having reached its pitiful zenith, had gone off to hide, leaving behind a change in the weather. Wind sounded in Harrek's sensors and drops of rain spotted his visor. A glance at the cruiser showed a well-bundled-up Lisa Marquez asleep in the front seat. It appeared that she had torn apart the troublesome forward fan: covered with a plastic sheet, its pieces lay bunched on the ground near the cruiser's nose. Harrek clanked past, eyes and filters adjusting to the darkness, greater hands feeling the way.

He made good time trudging up the nearest hill and down the other side. Frequently he stopped to examine a curious artifact or an example of native flora. Just as frequently he stopped to regain his balance—most disturbing, since he was supported by the structure of his sortie suit and therefore an attack of vertigo, to be so noticeable, had to be quite serious. It forced Harrek to review possible causes, and to reach no worthwhile conclusion. The only likely reason for his sudden illness was too terrifying to consider . . .

In the darkness he waded across a shallow creek, much to the dismay of several small, furry beings nearby, who grew quite agitated at his passage. Apparently they feared damage to a stick-and-mud barrier they had erected not far upstream. They did not attack, however, and Harrek was grateful. Even though he was deliberately courting death by fleeing from Boroz, he had no intention of making his final gift to Entropy at the claws of savage Earth aborigines.

After Harrek had spent an hour without another spell of vertigo, his customary optimism began to return. Perhaps it was merely the strain of travel at that, not some Earth virus, not his decision to forego his anti-rashch injections. He began to believe once again that he had been right to escape from Boroz and her cronies, who would have been content to let him remain Second forever. Harrek was aware that he had been accepted for the mission because Boroz wished to appear enlightened to certain factions. The inclusion of a lone Second in the group would go far toward appeasing the disgruntled mass of Seconds who viewed the mission to Earth as nothing more than a new way for the Firsts to enrich themselves and strengthen their hold on the Seconds. Harrek also knew that by taking him along Boroz prevented him from scheming and making trouble on Ashentar in her absence.

Harrek strongly suspected that Boroz did not wish him ever to return to Ashentar, especially since a heroic return would automatically elevate him to First. Accidents were easy to arrange on these exploratory missions.

All that would change soon. California awaited Harrek with its humans hungry for the knowledge of the Hocq, which he would gladly provide in exchange for sanctuary . . .

A foggy, mistlike rain began to fall, a rain very different from that of Ashentar. Harrek was tiring, and with the ground becoming muddy and unpassable, he concluded that he should return to camp. By going to his right he would eventually reach it.

He had not gone far when he heard sounds that could only be those of humans. He halted and, motionless, looked through the mist, into the spaces between the dark trees.

Immediately in front of him was a road, torn and rutted by time, and now turning to mud as well. Beyond lay a grove of dense vegetation, and in that grove Harrek perceived a cluster of buildings. He noted two heat sources—open fires—which were not directly visible but nevertheless gave unmistakable signatures to his sensors. He also detected two cooler sources which he judged to be machines recently in use. Finally he noted the presence of six moving, human-sized heat sources, and a trio of much larger ones.

These creatures and their camp lay directly between Harrek and safety. The rain thickened, growing louder as it drummed on his helmet. The ambient temperature continued to drop toward freezing. He recalled another storm, another time, on another world . . . on the Beggar's Plain during a storm of sixes. Then, too, he had been far from shelter and alone.

He made up his mind. He could skirt this human campsite with ease, the storm hiding the noise of his passage, the darkness sparing the natives the sight of him. He turned again and moved slowly along the edge of the road until the dangerous grove was out of sensor range. Possibly he could cut into the woods here . . .

He noted a new heat source, very close this time.

He had no time to wonder at its ability to approach without detection, for it was soon clear that this heat source was cooling too quickly to sustain a living organism. Therefore it was a dead body. Not far ahead he found it.

The body was human, as he had expected, dead for several hours at least, apparently killed by butchering. A sharp instrument had been drawn across the major extremity—the neck—bleeding the human to death. Harrek flashed a light for the benefit of his camera, and for direct vision. Strange: there was less blood in evidence than one expected.

Carefully Harrek let his greater hands roam the body as he whispered appropriate phrases from the songs of Entropy. He felt that the body should be taken to Lisa Marquez, who would surely know what to do with it, but when he tried to lift it he found it too heavy.

He dropped the body and almost fell over as his sickness returned in all its glory. Flailing about for balance, he hurtled into the woods and up the slope, no longer worried about stealth, because he was now sure what was causing his illness. He cursed himself for his ignorance, and for his bad luck.

Stumbling into camp, he orbited the cruiser helplessly, wondering how he would ever attract the attention of the sleeping Lisa Marquez. In frustration, as a second brutal wave of vertigo washed over him, he pounded all four hands on the cruiser.

She opened the door immediately. "Okay, okay! What's wrong?" He could only croak in reply.

"Let me get you inside, Harrek."

Somehow they made it to his tent. Once inside the pressure chamber he was able to regain his wits.

"You aren't well, Harrek. What can I do? Tell me."

Her concern touched him, making it even more painful for him to admit his problem. "My rashch approaches. It isn't supposed to occur now. I apologize."

The meaning of his statement didn't escape her. "You're *pregnant?* You're going to fission right *here?* When?"

"Soon. Perhaps within a day or two."

She smiled but even Harrek's limited exposure to humans told him there was no humor in it. "Well, I guess I should quit working on the car and boil some water." She left, leaving a miserable Harrek alone in his tent to contemplate the skewed mess of his carefully constructed worldline.

CHAPTER 11

Dubuque, Central States, Thursday Morning

"Well, folks, we'll be arriving at the Dubuque airport in about twenty minutes. It'll be a short stop, so those of you getting off here should be ready to move."

Strauss woke up at the driver's announcement. He plucked the pickup from his left ear and shut off his lap computer, which rested on the seat next to him. He stretched, looking at the dark Iowa countryside as it slipped past, perfectly content to savor his few remaining quiet moments. Being a civil servant had its advantages, especially if, like Strauss, you were a fairly royal civil servant. Travel was certainly easy to arrange. Yesterday Strauss had taken a government helicopter to the Austin airport, where his diplomatic pass freed two seats on the next shuttle to Oklahoma City. That second seat was normally intended for an assistant, but Strauss preferred to travel alone: he had a flunky waiting for him already. Besides, the computer provided all the backup he needed.

At Oklahoma City he had made connections with one of the few passenger lines still serving the CSA—Midwest—for the trip to Des Moines, which was surprisingly quick and trouble-free. A CSA official had met him at Des Moines and steered him through customs toward the bus, which would take its place in the evening convoy heading toward Dubuque. That had been six hours ago.

Strauss pried himself out of his seat, reminded once again that he needed to lose some weight. His dozen or so fellow passengers looked like farmers—agrifactory managers in their company uniforms. Yet no one had made Strauss feel unwelcome, in spite of the residual bitterness between their two nations. The five states of Great Texas, rich and warm, ruthlessly dominating everything between the Missouri border and the Panama Canal . . . and the chilly states of the CSA, whose survival depended on a growing season that grew shorter and shorter every year. These men had the same permanent sunburn—and pessimistic mask—that Strauss associated with Texan ranch hands. He was glad he hadn't tangled with them.

When he returned to his seat, decently awake if not entirely clean or refreshed, the driver was stopping the bus at a checkpoint. They were just outside the city proper now. The sky was growing bright. Strauss rubbed the fog off his window and strained to see . . . but, really, he wondered, what was there to see?

Shapiro waited in front of the tiny terminal building as Strauss got off the bus. With dark stubble around his mustache and his eyes blinking furiously, the second secretary had clearly not slept for days. Good, Strauss thought. "Boroz is anxious to see you," Shapiro said.

"She'll have to stay anxious for a while," Strauss snapped. "It took her ten years to get to this point; fifteen more minutes won't kill her." The sudden exposure to cold air took his breath away, shocking him into full wakefulness with the realization that he was not dressed for this weather. He allowed Shapiro, wrapped in an obviously borrowed overcoat, to hold the door for him as he hurried inside.

The terminal was all but deserted at this hour. A lone travel agent shuffled sleepily through papers at a counter between sips of what smelled like real coffee, while a pair of uniformed guards, roused out of their warm beds for the Hocq arrival, sulked nearby. Strauss was grateful, at least, that he would not have to contend with a crowd. Boroz would keep him busy enough.

"Is this still a functioning airport?" Strauss said.

"Mostly military and cargo. Believe me, you were safer on the bus," Shapiro said. He nodded toward a grimy corridor. "We're getting set up over here."

"Where is everybody?"

"The Governor and the rest of the Hocq are on their way to Minneapolis."

"The Africans, too?"

"I think so. We brought Boroz here from Chicago in one of the cruisers."

"That must have been enjoyable."

Shapiro didn't even react. "If the Africans or Russians got here, it was on their own."

After running another gauntlet of sleepy soldiers they reached the Dubuque command post of the Texas Rangers—an office containing two metal desks with comsoles, several well-worn chairs, and a large hanging map of Iowa that still showed pre-War boundaries. Strauss glanced at the copyright date: 1995, over forty years old. He laughed. "Where's Boroz now?"

"Still in the cruiser. Jensen's with her, trying to adapt one of the sortie units so she can get out and around."

Strauss rubbed his arms, hoping to start some circulation there, and wished for something hot to drink. "Why the hell do they have to adapt one?"

"She's too big for the standard model that was worked up for the other Hocq. It was some protocol thing, I guess. Boroz refused to let the Africans bring one along for her or even build one because she had no plans to 'walk with the animals.' "

"They'd save everybody a lot of trouble if they'd just use their own toys."

"Well, that's the whole problem, isn't it?"

Part of Shapiro's brain was still awake after all. "Good point, Doug. They're so goddamn afraid the wrong party's going to learn their little secrets." He accepted a cup of rose-scented tea, the first definite odor he had noticed in Iowa, one he was sure to associate with this place from now on. Warming his hands on the cup, he looked at the map. "Okay, tell me all the news."

Shapiro cleared his throat. "According to the regional commander, all evidence indicates that Marquez and the missing Hocq went down in *that* area"— he made a circle with his finger, pointing to the region immediately east of a city called Waterloo—"two nights ago. They say they even picked up a transponder blip about that time, though nothing since. I haven't seen any hard evidence myself; I'm just taking their word."

"I don't suppose anyone's asked for a spy satellite image."

"We don't have anything in the sky here and the military people I talked to were reluctant to divert one without the Governor's express order. Besides, it's cloudy."

"What about the CSA?"

"They don't have any."

"So the bottom line is, there's been no contact that we can confirm since Sunday night, and this is Thursday morning."

"Yes."

Strauss sipped at his tea. It tasted horrible, but it was hot. "Maybe all we're searching for is wreckage."

It was clear from his reaction that Shapiro hadn't thought of that. "I know it's unpleasant, Doug, but we can't rule out any possibility."

"I guess not."

"Has the regional commander got his troops out?"

"Yes, two battalions deployed in a standard quarantine, blocking and controlling all major roads into, out of, and around the target area. Aerial surveillance is continuing, starting at the quarantine perimeter and proceeding toward the center. Ground troops will converge on the center, too."

"How long will it take to reach the target?"

Shapiro closed his eyes and thought. Strauss could almost see him moving his lips. "Let's see . . . the troops are probably all on the road by now—"

"On the road? What the hell have they been doing since yesterday?"

Shapiro looked uncomfortable. "They're short on vehicles, especially aircraft, and they say they've had a lot of outlaw activity in the target area lately, which means that their rapid-deploy units are already rapidly deployed, in the wrong places. We've hardly been quick to respond ourselves."

"Conceded. Any more bad news?"

"The weather report isn't promising. They're expecting several inches of snow later today, so we can assume that the troops are going to move even slower."

"I can't believe it's all that tough for a unit out on a bandit hunt to redeploy for a simple quarantine."

"Well . . . there was a political problem that had to be solved before they would even think of moving."

Strauss grinned. "I wondered what caused the delay."

"The Governor spent part of Monday and all day Tuesday just convincing the mayor of Chicago and the Africans to guarantee some sort of aid to the CSA, in return for their sending out troops where and when we need them."

"No cash, no search."

"Well, it wasn't cash . . ."

"I know, trade credits. Oil and electric. It's still money to me, the cheap bastards. What are they charging us?"

"They haven't given us final figures yet—"

"Great. We're in cost-plus."

"—but we can count on spending at least two-point-five million on a three-day operation. The clock started at 6 P.M. yesterday and it's pro rata for overtime."

"At least they don't get golden time." Strauss sighed. "This is great. It's the goddamn Africans' fault that Marquez and the alien got away in the first place and now not only do we have to find the two of them, we've got to pay for the pleasure. You know the Africans and the Soviets will stall on the bill until the twenty-second century and we'll get stuck with it because we're their neighbors, which the CSA knows. Ruthven should have offered to bill the CSA for every stupid farmer who decides to come south this winter." He set his cup aside. "Well, they said the job was tough when we took it. So what have we got? Are we still pretending to call this a kidnapping? Have our Chicago comrades given us *anything* we can use?"

"They say they have no evidence of any involvement by known political terrorist groups."

"Which still leaves criminal terrorist groups. Any ransom demands?"

"No."

"I'm not surprised. I doubt that a hood could get his hands on a Hocq, even in Chicago. It looks like your plain old everyday defection."

"And that gives us a whole new set of problems. The news people."

"Christ, I forgot about them," Strauss said, having done nothing of the sort. But the admission of an oversight on his part would do wonders for Shapiro's morale: the guy was feeling beaten up. "Who do we have?"

"The press pool traveling with the Hocq."

"Africans and Russians? I think we can rely on their governments to make them see reason."

"There are American reporters in the pool, some from the CSA and even a crew from California."

Strauss didn't like that at all. "I see. I hope no one in our office had anything to do with accrediting those people."

"It was the Africans. I guess they were trying to buy some good-will for the conference in L.A."

"What does the press know so far?"

"Everyone in the pool knows that Harrek is missing. The guy from the CSA, through his contacts here, seems to know everything I've just told you, including the fact that you've been called in. I suspect that's all been passed on to the Californians by now."

"Am I going to have to tell these folks the facts of life?"

Shapiro finally smiled. "I don't think that is required just yet. They're all willing to play along, for the moment. It's the usual deal: in exchange for a temporary blackout, they get total access."

"And the whole story leaks five minutes after the first background briefing." Strauss rubbed his eyes. He didn't want to deal with the press. "Well, it always happens like that. Okay, they're in, but make them pay their own way. Better yet, encourage them to hit on the CSA for rides. It might be fun to watch some of those hotshots from L.A. trying to hustle these farmers for free wheels."

"All they have to do is put them on the network news."

"Good point, but don't let them push you around, Doug. This is very serious business. If we can get Harrek back and keep Boroz and the rest of them happy at the same time, it could mean a lot, if and when the Hocq finally decide to license the Genesis stuff. If it goes in the toilet, the fact that it's all the Africans' fault or that it started in Chicago isn't going to save us. We're going to be shut out. I'm sure I don't need to tell you what that's likely to do to you and me."

"I know," Shapiro said.

"I know you know. I'm just thinking out loud." He got busy at one of the comsoles, accessing some data which scrolled up on the screen. This was normally the sort of work an assistant could perform, but Strauss had worked his way through Texas Christian doing inputs, and he had yet to meet the secretary who was faster or better. He tried to connect with the Great Texas net but the comsole rejected the codes. The nationwide computer grid had fallen on hard times. "Suppose Marquez went off the deep end," he said suddenly.

Shapiro took a moment to reply. "I could order a psych model. We could have it in a couple of hours."

"I ordered my own yesterday and read it on the trip up. It's too goddamn ambiguous—those models always are. It showed that she was under a certain amount of stress, but not an unusual amount. General loyalty indexes were down, but not dangerously so. Besides, you know how useful that is. I'd hate to see mine after a bad day. To top it off, the model was based on an evaluation now four months old, otherwise known as almost completely worthless." He leaned back on the chair and rubbed his bald spot. He needed to get through to his computer. Maybe if he used his lap model . . . "And of course we can't even begin to evaluate the state of mind of Señor Harrek. It's possible he just up and decided it was time for a walk in the woods. Or maybe he didn't like the carpet in his hotel room. See if you can get hold of that Kenyan exopsychologist who was on the original contact team—"

"Oh no," Shapiro said.

Strauss had noticed a growing commotion outside the office. He got up and went to the door in time to see two of the local gendarmes backing down the corridor, retreating before a massive four-armed creature in a silver pressure suit. Boroz advanced until she loomed over Strauss. A distorted voice squawked from the chest pack on the alien's suit. "Here," Strauss said. Without hesitation he reached out and adjusted the gain on the speaker.

"What are you doing to find my unfortunate brother?" Boroz said loudly. "I demand information." The alien's adopted voice held an unusual mixture of twangy Texas cracker with the exaggerated, precise diction of an African lord.

Strauss glanced at the crowd which was forming at a discrete distance. "Excellency, could you step inside my office?"

It was a preposterous maneuver, but the alien managed to squeeze through the door by bending almost double, poking her head inside, and pushing and pulling around the corner with both pairs of arms. Strauss had seen Boroz once before, at the Hocq's first landing in Texas a year ago. He had watched from the stand as the thirteen aliens paraded from the modified Antonov-99 transport plane to the reception area through a transparent tunnel. They had been without pressure or sortie suits and, garbed in their native clothing, which consisted of colorful shirts and arm wrappings, looked more like four-armed, lizard-skinned old ladies on their way to a Havana vacation than mysterious aliens from Tau Ceti IV. It was undeniable that the suits added a certain element of ferocity and intimidation. And Boroz was clearly the most ferocious and intimidating of the Hocq.

"How can I make you comfortable, Excellency?"

"I am perfectly comfortable in this position," Boroz replied, standing just inside the door with her helmet scraping the ceiling, her lower arms folded awkwardly at her side. The Ambassador obviously had a sense of humor.

Strauss closed the door. "I don't know how much Mr. Shapiro has told you, Excellency, but we have managed to narrow down—"

"It is imperative that Harrek be returned immediately."

"—as I was saying, Excellency, we expect to have your brother—"

"This entire mission is in jeopardy. There will be no Genesis dispersal until Harrek is returned. There will be no Genesis dispersal at all if Harrek is not returned safely and immediately."

"I can assure you that my government is well aware of that, Excellency." Boroz must have been taking negotiating lessons from the Soviets. Strauss turned to Shapiro, who was wedged unhappily in the corner. "Doug, you're excused. Please see to those matters we discussed." Gratefully, Shapiro left. Strauss wished he'd been able to offer the younger man some encouragement. After all, no one on the Governor's staff had been executed for incompetence for a decade; not even the general services administration computers would hold Shapiro responsible for this mess. They'd save that pleasure for

Strauss. "It's very likely, Excellency, that your brother has been kidnapped or otherwise coerced into—"

"I'm aware of the matrix of options," Boroz said. "I can only repeat that Harrek must be recovered immediately and that I must be present. There is no further discussion. This is a religious matter."

Religious matter! No doubt Cortez told the Aztecs it was a "religious matter" when his men deserted to find their own fortunes among the Incas. Strauss was fast losing his awe of the Hocq, though he was coming to appreciate their deviousness.

"Let's talk about that, Excellency."

CHAPTER 12

Outlaw Territory, Thursday Morning

"Jeremy, can you come here a moment?" Lisa raised her head out of the open fan cowling. Now where was he?

She'd found him waiting when she crawled out of the cruiser little more than an hour ago. After getting over the initial shock she realized she didn't mind having him around. And with the pieces of the fan so cold and wet that her fingers were already numb, she could certainly use a helping hand or two. Harrek's distressing news made her happy those hands were human. Besides, this kid liked machines! Over breakfast he'd told her about some silly wind generator he'd tried to fix, which showed that he was bright and ambitious, if a bit unlucky.

For the last half hour, though, he'd been sitting in the front seat of the Hurricane, playing with the comm unit.

"Jeremy!" Lisa called a second time. There he was. "Good. Grab that branch and pull when I give you the word. I've got most of the other Mississippi gunk cleaned out of here by now, but that damned branch is still stuck. So you pull and I'll pry . . ." Bending to work, she promptly rapped her knuckles on a sharp edge inside the housing. The pain and frustration brought real tears to her eyes.

"Here." Jeremy was holding out his gloves. "Looks like you need these more than I do."

"I think you're right," she said. With warm hands she was able to wedge a socket handle behind the fan without further damage to herself. She hollered, "Now!" Jeremy gave a good tug, and the branch came away in two pieces.

She made quick work of the reassembly from that point on, having done little but fool around with the various parts these last few days. Finally she was able to close the housing. She latched it and stood up, her forehead damp. Her lower back hurt, too, but she was determined not to let it bother her. "That just might do the trick," she said, handing Jeremy his gloves. "Thank you."

"Glad I could help." He fumbled for words. "I, ah, suppose you'll be leaving pretty soon now."

"God, I hope so. I should have been in Denver yesterday."

"Do you have room for another passenger?"

Surprise! she thought. "Jeremy, why on earth would you want to come with Harrek and me?"

She expected him to look away, as would a shy teenager, but he didn't. The only sign of nervousness was his tugging at an earlobe. For the first time she realized that this was not just some impulsive farm kid . . . there were lines in that young face, some gray hair around that stocking cap, traces of an old scar on one cheek. She was reminded of the old notion that people grew up fast in the country. "I told you what it's like here," he said. "There's no future. There isn't a hell of a lot of present, come to think of it. I can't live here anymore, and if I'm going to help the others, I've got to get out." He made a little gesture with his hand that seemed to say that "out" meant "anywhere but here."

In a way, knowing nothing of importance about Jeremy's family life, Lisa understood his need to escape. The morning—cold, gray, and depressing—was the sort of middle American day she'd always imagined but never experienced. It made her head ache so badly that the thought of another day here, much less a lifetime, made her suicidal. Add to that the burden of a neo-pioneer lifestyle and constant hunger, and the knowledge that there was something better just down the road . . . well, the lucky ones were those who had the guts to get out.

But not with her, unfortunately, not with Harrek. "Look," she said finally, "I still have to test this thing. Want to come along?"

"Sure." He gave no indication that he took this offer as a promise of more.

"Climb in."

Once in the cockpit, she showed Jeremy how to belt in. He followed instructions well and settled back, unperturbed. Lisa wanted to feel as relaxed as he looked. She started the engines, slowly revved them up to takeoff speed. No redlines. Up they went.

As the Hurricane rose into the sky, Lisa glanced at Jeremy. No white knuckles. Good for him.

At four hundred feet she throttled back to 60 percent, with all four fans spinning. Everything on the dash was still green, so she put the cruiser in a gentle climb.

"I haven't told you how much I appreciate your help," she said. "I never could have gotten that branch out of there without your help."

"You could have used Harrek."

At a thousand feet they picked up some buffeting, but nothing to worry about. The guidance system kept them level. "Only as a last resort," she said. "He's nocturnal and I hate to wake him up in the middle of the night." She wanted to add, He's pregnant and unpredictable and I want to stay as far away from him as possible!

"Wouldn't he offer to help? He wants to get to Denver, too, doesn't he?"

She laughed. "Jeremy, the Hocq—how can I explain this?—the Hocq don't think like we do. You and I would pitch in and help, but the Hocq are used to having human beings looking after them. At least that's what we've been doing ever since they got here, and that's six years now."

"Sounds strange to me."

"Waiting on the Hocq hand and foot? Boy, you *have* been out in the woods. Don't you know about the Genesis File?" His expression made it obvious he did not.

She couldn't keep the sarcasm out of her voice. "Why, my boy, the Genesis File could be the most important thing that ever happened to the human race! It's the collection of superknowledge that the Hocq have brought us . . . sort of a CARE package from the rest of the galaxy. You know, information that will tell us how to eliminate hunger, cure cancer, and balance checkbooks in a single bound. And if you believe all that, I've got some Brownsville real estate for you."

She realized how silly she sounded and shut up. She was filthy and worried and in desperate need of a good night's sleep—in a bed. And all she had to look forward to was a gauntlet run to Denver.

They were high enough now to see the rooftops of West Union. Time for the big test. Lisa enabled the guidance system to rev all four fans in all possible combinations, throttling up to 100 percent power on each. Everything stayed green. She lost altitude and started a wide turn back toward the campsite. There was no sense wasting fuel here, though she knew she had nowhere near enough to reach Denver. That was tomorrow's problem. She wished, however, that she had more flying time in the Hurricane. She would need the experience when she went buzzing across strange, rugged countryside tonight.

"I'm sorry, Jeremy. I'm getting cranky. There is a Genesis File, all right. I didn't believe it at first, but I've seen enough evidence to become a believer. The Hocq are keeping it to themselves for reasons known only to God. So everyone on Earth—except for you, I guess —has been trying to figure out what it will take to convince them to release it. At the very least, you'd want to be around when they do."

"And that's why you're with Harrek."

"Is it? I suppose it looks like that . . ."

An alarm sounded on the dash. "Now what the hell could that be?" Her first worried thought was the number three fan, but scanning the readouts she saw no problems. She told the computer to evade, and the cruiser promptly wrenched into a tight turn that shoved Lisa and Jeremy deep into their seats and gave Jeremy his first straight-down look at the ground . . . two thousand feet below him. The one-eighty turn stopped and they were at tree level. Lisa checked the radar.

She saw three blips at two thousand feet in the direction of West Union. As she watched, the blips seemed to climb, then peel away in different directions. The alarm annunciator shut off. Lisa asked the computer for identification on the blips.

HELICOPTERS, the computer replied.

Whose? she queried.

TRANSPONDERS OF CENTRAL STATES MILITARY COMMAND. ARMAMENT INCLUDES MISSILES AND BLAZERS. DEPLOYING IN BASIC SEARCH PATTERN—

Shaking all the way, Lisa let the computer fly them at treetop level back to camp. Once on the ground she drove the cruiser as close to the ancient farmhouse as she could, hoping to keep it invisible from the air. In silence she and Jeremy watched the radar screen as the choppers dropped off, having given no sign that they had detected the cruiser. Lisa was grateful for the cloudy day.

She started to relax again, but only momentarily. This was a new complication. She had been prepared to outrun a police helicopter or two, but now she was going to have to evade three military aircraft and all their support systems . . . on limited fuel. She considered surrender, but had to reject it. She could not abandon Harrek to the dubious mercies of the People's Republic, not to mention his sister Boroz. They weren't that desperate . . . yet.

"Well, Jeremy, now you can see what Harrek and I are facing. We're fugitives."

"Who's chasing you? The bluejackets?"

"Central States? They're in it, too, but it's mainly Texans and Chicagoans. And Russians and Africans."

"It's Harrek they want?"

"That's right. They'd *like* to get me, I imagine, but Harrek is the important one. You see, it's very likely that there's going to be another war, this one between Texas and California, especially if Texas gets hold of the Genesis File. All that superknowledge will give them superweapons, and my people have never been able to resist the chance to try out superweapons. The only way I can prevent a war is to get Harrek to the other side, so they get the File."

"The Californians won't use it?"

"Oh, they're just as bad as the Texans, but they won't be able to keep it secret the way the Texans would. If California gets the File, pretty soon the whole world gets it. If nothing else, maybe I'll have helped postpone the inevitable."

"It's hard for me to imagine that. A war between Texas and California, I mean."

"Not for me, unfortunately." She remembered the sky over Brownsville during those weeks, filled with smoke from the fires that consumed the bodies of plague victims. She had been ten years old.

"Look, Jeremy, I'm probably crazy, thinking I can affect world events. But you can help your family and friends, that's where you have to start." She rummaged in a storage compartment and produced a thin, gold-colored box the size of an open hand. "Here," she said, giving it to Jeremy. "You liked playing with the comm unit. This is a portable version. It'll tie in to the world satellite nets. You can get TV, radio, databases, the works. The batteries are probably good for five years. If you can't use it, you can take it to that store in West Union and get some cash for it. Consider it a gift. I wish I could stick around and teach you how to use it."

He took it carefully. "I'm used to teaching myself. Thank you."

"I suppose I'd better get some rest. I've got a lot of driving to do tonight." They got out of the cruiser.

"Good luck," Jeremy said. "And say good-bye to Harrek for me."

Lisa gave him a hug. "I will. And hey, if I get out of this mess, maybe I'll even come back for a visit. Bring you some new batteries for the unit."

"Help me finish my wind machine."

"That's a deal. Now scoot. You'll be late for lunch."

With growing sadness, she watched him disappear into the woods. Once again she was alone, in trouble, kept company only by a sick, fugitive alien being.

Turning away, she shivered in the cold, then headed toward Harrek's tent.

CHAPTER 13

Arrowsmith, Thursday Afternoon

When he saw Ben and the wagon rattle toward him across the field, Jeremy wanted to turn and run. But by then it was too late. He kept digging as the wagon pulled up and stopped.

Ben didn't waste words. "Where the hell have you been?"

"Around," Jeremy said, setting his shovel aside. He had been working here in the north field, near the old highway, for an hour, since midday. He had carefully avoided the house on his return from the Quiller farm, figuring today would be a good day to catch up on long-neglected chores, like patching a hole in the fence line. Anything to take his mind off his other problems.

"Around," Ben repeated. "That could mean anywhere." Carefully he got down from the wagon. "Elizabeth's been worried, you know. You weren't home at all yesterday and no one got a chance to see you this morning. Neil's been gone for the last two nights. Now, I know you're an adult and all that, but with things the way they are, it doesn't show much responsibility to be missing half the time." For the first time Ben looked directly at him. "Does it?"

"No, sir." Jeremy resumed digging, aware that chewing him out was always as unpleasant for Ben as it was for him.

"Well, then. I don't mean to be after you. I just want you to think about other people and their feelings. Neil's another matter," he added, shaking his head. He took a couple of slow steps and surveyed Jeremy's work. "Let me help you with that." He reached for a board, lifting one end.

The summer rains had eaten away the hillside here, washing out a section of fence. The hole had to be fixed before the ground froze, before the runoff next spring had a chance to make it worse. In the space of an hour Jeremy had completed the basic landscaping and erected a new fence post. All that remained was to connect cross-beams to the surviving posts on either side. Ben held while Jeremy quickly nailed them home.

"You're getting handier with that thing," Ben kidded. Long ago Jeremy had thumped his finger with a hammer and his "clumsiness" had become a community joke. "Dan was asking about you."

"What's bothering him now?"

"I went down to Sun House yesterday to tell him about those tracks you found, and of course he got all excited. He had Cory dig out the old bazooka or some damn thing he found buried over to Elkader. He wants to talk to you as soon as you get time. I told him you were off working with Hugh. But that was yesterday."

"I *was* working with Hugh. Yesterday."

"Well, this morning Dan walked all the way up here looking for you, and nobody could tell him where you were. He got a little, well, you know, excited. Had some new job for you, too, I think."

"That figures. He's probably forgotten all about the tracks."

There was silence. Jeremy collected his tools and stuck the unused nails in his pocket. He could feel Lisa's gift—the comm unit—there.

"He isn't that bad," Ben said finally. "You can't remember Dan when he was younger, but he was about all that held this place together. People got lazy, he'd get after them. People got crazy, he kept them in line. Most of the time he was the only person had any idea what to do when we had problems. I seem to recall that he taught you to read, too. He goes back all the way, too. And if he gets a bit fuzzy now and then, well, we're all facing that someday. Though it'd be tough to convince you of that."

"At the rate we're going, I'll never get that far," Jeremy said bitterly.

"We've had trouble before—"

"Not like this!" Jeremy couldn't help himself. "Look, I know there were always people running away and outlaws coming through, and you never really had enough food—okay. But you *wanted* to keep the community alive. You were living here because it was *better* than living Outside."

"We're still here. People do have good days and bad days."

"We don't have people anymore. Can't you see that? When you were my age there must have been two hundred in Arrowsmith. Where did they all go? Half of them are in the ground now and the rest walked down that road and never looked back. Did you ever count the number of kids in the third generation? *Seven*—that's all that survived. How are we supposed to continue with that?"

"You should be the strong ones, then," Ben said quietly. "The toughest ones. You had to be tough to live this long. Pretty soon you won't have anyone around telling you how wonderful things were before the War. You can make your own world, your own way of living—"

Jeremy just shook his head. "Ben, you don't understand. The whole point of Arrowsmith is gone. It was a family . . . we were supposed to take care of each other because no one outside would. But it hasn't happened that way. No one believes it anymore. We aren't any better than outsiders. In some ways we're a hell of a lot worse." He was trembling with conviction, never having said such things out loud to Ben before, and with fear, afraid of the reaction. "For years we've all been saying we believe in 'principles but not establishments,' but all I see right now is a commune without people."

But Ben held his temper. He only coughed once. Jeremy sensed that it was time to cool things off. "How are you feeling?" he asked.

"Old," Ben answered. "I've still got this damned cough and I just can't seem to get my breath a lot of the time. There are days when it doesn't bother me too much . . ." He shrugged, tapping his hand on the side of the wagon. The horse muttered. "Let me tell you something, Jeremy," Ben said suddenly. "You can say and think what you want, and God knows you can pretty much do what you want. No one's got the muscle to stop you. If you want to march down that road there, well, go ahead and do it. But don't tell me it's because *we* aren't a family any more. You'll be the one walking away from responsibilities. You get them when you're born, that's part of the deal. I'm not talking about me and your mother, either. I mean the girl and her baby. Just you think about *them* before you make any big decisions. Make sure it's something that's going to be best for them, not just you. If you want to be believing in something." He tried to smile, to take the sting out of what he said. "We all need to remember that."

Jeremy knew right then that he wasn't going down the road. Ben knew him too well, knew just what to say. He could get as angry as he wanted at Dan or Cissy or bad luck, but he couldn't hate them enough to divorce himself from the family.

He helped Ben back into the wagon. "Where are you going?"

"I thought I'd take a drive over to Brandy's," Ben said, "see if she knows where Neil might be. It isn't like him to stay out of touch for so long."

"Want me to come along?"

"No, I think it would be best if you went by the house and let Heather and Elizabeth know you're all right. While you're at it . . ."

Jeremy grinned. "I might just as well walk down the hill and see what Dan wanted."

"It would make things easier. People worry about you, you know. It's hard to miss those moods."

"Okay." He watched Ben drive away, then turned and started toward Hill House. As he did he took the comm unit out of his pocket. What an incredible piece of machinery! And what good would it do him now?

Before he reached the house he tossed it far into the field.

What was wrong with the greenhouse? Dan Aucheron took his cracked eyeglasses out of his pocket and put them on. He had noticed the unusually chilly air as soon as he came through the big double doors, but had not been certain, at least for a moment, if there were truly a problem, or if it were just an old man's circulation that gave him the chill. No, he could see now the telltale brown edges on the leaves, and they did feel dry to the touch. He moved to another tree . . . its leaves, too, were brittle and spotted with yellow. Even the bark felt cold, which told Dan that the trees had been exposed for more than a single night. He looked around and saw, high up, a broken window. Well now, that sort of thing happened. Sometimes birds would smash into the greenhouse with such force that they punched right through the glass. Then you were supposed to tell Ben Clayton, so that he might talk a new sheet of glass out of Kelleher, or you took yourself over to Elkader and liberated a replacement from the ruins. In the meantime you crawled up there and boarded over that hole so your plants didn't freeze. You just didn't *leave* it!

He kicked an empty flower pot across the floor with such force that it shattered against the wall. The noise should have attracted the attention of at least a pair of community members, but no one appeared. Dan was alone in the place, kept company only by frozen trees and the whistling wind.

Where were they? Dan found the blackboard that listed the work rotation, but it had been wiped clean, which didn't surprise him. Cissy Funderburk had been neglecting her responsibilities of late, anyway. In fact, it was Dan's suspicions of her that brought him out to the greenhouse this morning. But the community didn't dance to the tune of any single person. There were others he would want to confront. He went back outside, squinting in the light, and started across the cold yard toward the barn that stood just below New House.

In spite of today's problem, Dan Aucheron was happier than he had been in years, happiness being defined as a state when, in the lifeless quiet of the night, you still looked forward to morning. There had been times in his life when he had not felt that eagerness, when he had lain awake not caring if the sun came up. It had happened with increasing frequency since their most recent siege of troubles began. But, on the whole, he was happy now . . . and he didn't know quite why. It wasn't because of the weather, which was mostly depressing; it wasn't on account of his health, which was neither remarkably good nor remarkably bad; it surely wasn't because of the current state of the commune.

There was a tune playing in his head these days, a fragment of a song that had played endlessly on the wonderful stereo that once covered a wall of the common room in New House. A song about a "child of God" who was "walking along the road" to a place called Woodstock. The tune took him back sixty summers . . .

It was on July 31, 1970, that Phillip James Aucheron, age thirty-two, and Danielle Freeman-Aucheron, age thirty-one, of Cambridge, Massachusetts, closed escrow on a run-down farm here in the bluff country west of the Mississippi, just a few miles outside the city of Elkader, Iowa. For the grand total of $9,500 cash, plus change, in the form of a cashier's check drawn on the Bank of America and handed to Mr. Dougherty of Elkader First Farmer's (who processed the necessary papers with great speed), Phillip and Danielle became the proud owners of sixty-five acres of what was euphemistically known as "marginal" farmland, at the intersection of Highway 56 and Arrowsmith Road. The inventory gave them one two-story, three-bedroom house (including indoor plumbing); one proven well; and two outlying structures in different states of decrepitude. There was no livestock, though the bank had leased some of the upper field for grazing. The fields, if one could safely call them that, had borne their last cash crop during the middle years of the Eisenhower administration, at which time the last owner, a Mr. Azel Gutenberg, died intestate, and without heirs.

The few neighbors looked upon the arrival of the newcomers from "back East" with indifference that slid all too easily into outright hostility. The Aucherons spoke with the flat "ah" and missing terminal R of suburban Boston, which was not, in itself, an accent completely different from the rural Iowanese of their neighbors . . . but Phillip wore his hair to his shoulders and his beard Old Testament bushy while Danielle usually went barefoot and didn't shave her legs. They dressed like farmers, in overalls and work shirts, while the real farmers kept their hair trimmed and wore madras sportcoats and white shoes to Saturday golf and Sunday church. It was rumored that the two weren't legally married. They didn't bother to get a telephone. They probably grew and smoked marijuana. They kept their eight-year-old son Daniel out of public and parochial school (which brought a man from the school district around from time to time; he didn't want to turn a truancy into a federal case, and had no need, once Danielle produced her Massachusetts teaching certificate and M.F.A. sheepskin). They seemed to live on love or money from heaven, since they did no serious farming. Betting around the golf-club bar was that these two didn't even know where the elevator was . . . yet they always had some sort of weird construction project going, self-contracted, too, the results of which or attempts at which could be seen from the highway.

There was one incident at Sweet Corn Days that first summer when Phillip and a local yokel got into an argument about the Vietnam War, which ended with the citizen calling Phillip "a goddamn hippie" while Phillip walked away in a hurry.

But mostly they were left alone. In that they considered themselves luckier than their friends back East, who were still battling the traffic on the Monsignor O'Brien Highway, still breathing the smog, still busing their kids to the South Side, still buying deadbolts for the doors.

Besides, there were some advantages. This region sat on the edge of the best farmland in the country, and probably the world. The climate, while harsher than they would have liked, nevertheless provided sufficient rainfall and at least average sunshine. There would be only a single growing season, but it was usually a good one—and not one subject to frequent catastrophes such as drought and heat, which is what you found farther south in Kansas or Oklahoma. A good average wind speed meant that windpower was a workable alternative energy source someday. There was timber nearby, and wildlife, of a sort: beaver and fox, for example.

All of this, of course, had been spelled out in the mimeographed Survival Guide Danielle had picked up at B.U. one day. The guide listed various zones in the United States which stood a good chance of escaping the firestorm of an all-out nuclear exchange, or the social upheaval that was sure to follow the upcoming revolution. The safest zones were not, as the Aucherons had supposed, in the Far West, because states like Colorado, Utah, Montana, and Arizona were choked with military bases and missile silos—certain targets when the nukes started to drop. It was a shame, because their dream hideout had been northern Arizona, with its sunshine, forests, and endless open spaces. New England—Maine and Vermont, that is—got high marks in the guide, but it struck Phillip and Danielle that life up there was always going to be cold, knotty, a never-ending struggle to scratch a living out of rock. But as the guide put it, "Check out this corner of Iowa. The glaciers missed it. Armageddon might, too."

So on summer break, 1969, Phillip and Danielle and Danny flew out to Chicago to visit friends, then rented a car and drove clear across Illinois, where they visited half a dozen towns listed in the guide, asking questions, taking pictures, camping out by the road, looking up at Armstrong and Aldrin on the Moon, dreaming. It was a beautiful summer, warm and alive, and they became convinced that here was a safe place to ride out the long, cruel winters ahead. Woodstock, later that summer, gave them further encouragement. Kent State, the following spring, pushed them over the edge.

Phillip sold his half of Aucheron-Bales Electronic Design and Danielle quit her teaching assistantship at B.U. They pooled their savings (which consisted largely of Danielle's small inheritance) and proceeds from the sale of their furniture. They bought copies of *The Whole Earth Catalog,* said good-bye to their friends (inviting them to follow when it looked like "it was all going down"), put little Danny in the VW, and headed out Interstate 12.

By March of '71 they had completely gutted the old farmhouse and redesigned it to accommodate a solar water-heating system that would not be installed for several years; they just knew they wanted one. They put new Owens-Corning insulation in the walls, ceilings, and floors, ordered an experimental Swedish-built toilet that was better than the common model because it didn't use water and combined waste with lime to make fertilizer, and, into the south side of the house, put special double-paned windows that would give maximum sunlight and warmth in December yet would provide excellent cooling in July and August, when they would be shaded by the overhanging roof.

It was Danny who started calling the place "New House."

In their worn-out fields they planted wheat, corn and alfalfa, just as the books said to. There was no possibility of a cash crop that year, if ever, but the fields needed "exercising" and that was the classic method. They laid out several huge gardens below New House that eventually would yield tomatoes, carrots, and potatoes. They planted apple trees and berry vines. At an auction they picked up a used John Deere tractor and tiller, which caused them endless headaches with maintenance and the purchase of gasoline, but eventually saved them hours. Besides, they had hardly renounced the internal combustion engine or reliance on the world oil cartels: they were still getting use out of the VW, and once drove all the way to Des Moines to see the Stones in concert.

And if the tractor gave only slightly more than it took, the by now regular visits of neighbors were an unquestioned bonus. Apparently the Iowans couldn't stand to see anyone—even "goddamn hippies" —making repeated farming mistakes. Danielle, the *de facto* agricultural specialist of the family (Phillip did all the construction work), had found to her dismay that you didn't learn farming from a book. She was grateful for the advice, and paid attention to it.

They acquired a puppy, several kittens (which were not allowed inside New House), a pig, two goats, several Rhode Island Reds, and a cow, and a horse . . . but slowly, because the idea was to have New House pay for itself, and because they wanted to feed the live-stock from what was grown on the farm. There was also some reluc-tance to burden themselves with too many creatures, since neither Phillip nor Danielle knew much about animal husbandry. But the chickens just about took care of themselves and the goats were ac-tively helpful, and the dog and cats provided hours of free amuse-ment. Danny, who had never been allowed to have a pet, took care of them all.

By August '72 Phillip was working the harvest up and down High-way 56, finding in return that he had a neighbor who was only too happy to bring his big International Harvester over to New House to get the hippies' crops in. The hot Friday that Dave Pratt came over he had a six-pack of Old Milwaukee stashed in the cab, and that eased considerably the misery of harvesting on a muggy day with the temperature in the nineties. Phillip turned Dave onto the last of their Boston stash, then showed him the hemp patch down by the creek bottom. That evening David's wife, Bonnie, came over, bringing their two kids, and they all wound up staying the weekend.

By mid-October the Pratt kids were living at New House while Dave and Bonnie, under Phillip's guidance, were converting their house and farm to this eastern hippie way of doing things.

It was Danny who called the Pratt place "Hill House."

Others began to move in. Margie and Suzanne, friends of Da-nielle's, stopped by on their way to Minneapolis that Christmas, and never did get back to Cambridge. A drifter named Billy Godsey, on

his way to Toronto to ride out the draft, decided New House might
be just as safe and not nearly as cold. And just after New Year's
1973, Russ Clayton showed up, fresh out of M.I.T. and looking for a
vacation before reporting to Hughes Aircraft in California.

By then the family—the "commune," Bonnie Pratt called it—had
fourteen members. And when the Pratts' third child, Sioux Anne,
was born it was understood that she would be raised by Margie and
Suzanne, since they were so good with kids, and because Bonnie was
spending a lot of her time building a greenhouse . . .

He made a misstep and stumbled, falling to his hands.

"Dan!" One of the women called to him. "Are you all right?"

It was Elizabeth Clayton, one of the second generation, a good
girl. "Fine," he said, waving her away, which of course did no good
at all.

"Are you sure?" Elizabeth said. She took off her backpack and
helped him stand up. "That path is terrible. I've taken a couple of
spills myself."

Dan smiled. Elizabeth hadn't stumbled since she learned how to
walk. "I'm fine," he insisted. "Just deteriorating in my own sweet
way."

"Oh, *Dan!* Where were you heading? I could walk with you."

"I should be the one asking that of such a pretty girl." Dan had
always had his eye on Elizabeth, right up till the time she moved in
with Ben Clayton . . . and maybe a little past that.

Elizabeth picked up her pack and gave him a sly smile. "You don't
sound too deteriorated to me. As a matter of fact, I was going back
to the Hill. Heather and I are doing some canning."

"No, no. I'm just looking for Hugh and Cory. I can find them
easily enough on my own."

Elizabeth seemed concerned, but said, "Okay. I'll see you later."
And she hurried off.

Dan continued on to the barn. As he reached it the side door
opened and big Hugh Walton came out. "Well! Hi there, Dan. How
are you today?"

"I need to talk to you, Hugh."

"Gee, Dan, I'm in a big hurry—"

The door opened again. This time it was Cory Turner, with two pieces of plywood under his arm, asking "Where's the hammer? Oh, hi, Dan. We were just on our way over to the greenhouse."

"That's what I came to talk about," Dan said. "The trees are dying up there . . ."

"They're cold, Dan," Hugh said, "but relax. They'll be all right. It takes more than one night of frost to—"

"There's nobody working up there!"

Cory looked to Hugh for help. "Dan," Hugh said, "there's nothing to be *done* right now. Even Cissy can tell you that she's got a lot more jobs than she does people. No one's got any time to waste on a bunch of trees that aren't going anywhere anyway."

"The window's broken," Dan repeated.

"We *know.*" Hugh rubbed his graying beard. "I saw it last night and Jeremy's coming down from the Hill any minute now to see how big the hole is and what he can do about finding something to fix it. He'll probably have it all taken care of by this time tomorrow. You know how he is about fixing things."

Dan suddenly felt tired and old. He was acting like a cranky old man. Hugh was nearly fifty . . . surely he didn't need Dan telling him how to do his job.

"What's Ben doing down here?" Cory pointed past them toward the driveway, which opened into Arrowsmith Road. Dan turned and saw Ben guide the wagon to a noisy halt. He climbed out, looking grim.

Hugh and Cory got to the wagon first. "What did you bring us this time?" Cory shouted, then shut up.

There was a body in the back of the wagon.

Hugh lifted the blanket that covered the still form. "Oh no," he said.

Dan pushed Cory aside so he could see. "That's Neil," he announced. "One of them from the Hill." The boy's face was frosted, muddy, twisted. His neck had been slashed and, from the looks of his clothing, he had been bled like a butchered hog. Very bad, Dan thought.

Cory ran for the barn.

Hugh let the blanket drop. "Where did you find him, Ben?"

"Down in the hollow a ways," Ben said. "Hold on." He was look-ing up the Hill. Following his glance, Dan saw Jeremy running to-ward them.

"Jeremy! Over here!" Hugh called. Jeremy arrived out of breath. "When was the last time you saw Neil?"

"Yesterday morning," Jeremy said. "Over at Brandy's. Why?" Sensing that something was terribly wrong, he pushed past them to the wagon and ripped away the blanket. After a moment he closed his eyes.

"Your daddy found him down near Brandy's, isn't that right, Ben?" Hugh said.

"About halfway between the highway and Brandy's place, actu-ally. Real close to the old Quiller farm, in fact."

Dan was pacing. "Who would do something like this?" he de-manded.

"Outlaws," Hugh announced firmly. "Jeremy's outlaws."

Of course! Dan thought. How could he have forgotten?

"That's a possibility," Ben said, keeping his eyes on Jeremy. "But we only know that outlaws passed through here yesterday. There were some very strange tracks near the body. I've never seen any-thing like them, that's for sure."

Cory rejoined them, still nervously wiping his sleeve across his mouth.

"What the hell took you down to the Quiller place?" Hugh asked.

Ben hesitated. "Oh, just exercising the horse a bit."

"Well," Hugh said, "what do we do now?"

"Bury the boy," Dan said. "That comes first. And take care of that hole in the greenhouse. You know, I went up there a little while ago and it was like winter—"

"We'll do that," Ben said quickly. "First thing. Cory, you take Jeremy and get that window fixed. Do it tonight or we'll be using those trees for firewood tomorrow. Hugh and I will see to Neil."

Cory seemed grateful for the assignment. He hefted his plywood and tools and started for the path up the Hill. Jeremy followed with-out comment.

Once they were gone, Ben said, "Will that do it?"

"Yes, yes," Dan said. "This is terrible for the younger ones, losing a friend this way. I remember when Crystal passed away—"

"Dan," Hugh said, "isn't it getting a little cold out for you?"

"Hmmm?" Yes, it *was* getting cold, and late, too. "Good idea. I'm going inside for some tea. How about you boys?"

"Not just yet," Ben said.

"Well, don't be too long." He headed for the house. Behind him Hugh and Ben kept talking about horses and strangers and riding around after dark. Dan didn't have much interest in that sort of thing anymore. He was happy that the greenhouse would be warm tonight.

Greatly comforted, he went into New House.

CHAPTER 14

Dubuque, Central States, Thursday Afternoon

Tim Strauss was on his way back from the men's room when Shapiro met him outside their "command post." "The Governor's on the phone," Shapiro said. "Teleconference. We can take it in the administrator's office."

With uncharacteristic decisiveness, Shapiro steered Strauss down the hall to a second office. This one, with its indirect lighting and gray tones, was a substantial improvement over the one given to the Texans. Then a heavy-set secretary showed them to the inner office, and even Strauss was impressed. "Now I know why the Central States can't afford to buy oil from us," he said softly. "Thank you, ma'am," he added to the secretary, who was showing them how to operate the expensive but ten-year-old system. "We know how to use the phone." She left.

Strauss sat down and dialed. "Has this been swept?" he asked Shapiro.

"Did it myself. It's clean."

"That's too bad, in a way. It might be instructive for some of the folks in these parts to hear how their leaders operate. Hello, Governor!"

Ruthven appeared in the left half of the screen set into the wall. "Mr. Bannekker will be picking up . . ." the Governor said. A moment later the African foreign minister appeared in the right half of the screen. Shapiro slipped out of the room.

Strauss quickly brought them up to date on the quarantine and search plans, finishing, "We'll be leaving here in about two hours and expect to have Harrek and Marquez in the bag by this time Friday."

"Good job, Tim," Ruthven said. "I don't have any questions. Mr. Bannekker?"

"I have a few. Is this line secure?"

"Yes, sir."

"Good. We received some rather disturbing intelligence reports about Dr. Marquez. Is it true that she was *born* in California?"

"Yes, sir," Strauss said. "Her family moved to Texas just before the War."

"According to our sources, she has maintained close personal contacts in California. I'm not free to divulge my sources"—Don't bother, Strauss wanted to say: we have our own agents inside your committee for state security—"but it appears that Marquez has made an unusual number of trips to California in the four years she has been on the Governor's staff—"

"Excuse me, Mr. Bannekker," Strauss said. He could see Ruthven shaking her head. "If you're looking for an admission from me that there has been a Texan security lapse, you've got it. We blew it. I've already admitted as much to Ambassador Boroz, if you're interested."

Bannekker seemed as surprised as he was satisfied. It was the damn File again. Every country was keeping score, making sure the Hocq knew of the other's failings. "But remember this," Strauss continued, "Marquez, no matter what her political beliefs, couldn't begin to carry out something like this without help. Harrek had to be the instigator. Which means to me that the Hocq themselves have suffered a security lapse . . . which means, I guess, that Texas and the Hocq have something in common."

Ruthven cleared her throat and changed the subject. "Captain Strauss has no way of knowing this, Mr. Bannekker. Tim, Texas and the Afro-Soviet Union have signed an accord which requires each to share in any potential Genesis license."

Strauss kept his face a mask. "Understood, Governor." His personal inclination was to do without the Genesis File rather than share it with the Africans and Russians. He guessed he just didn't understand politics.

"It won't be announced for several days yet," Bannekker said. "But it is a coup for both of us, given the collapse of the California conference. Who knows what wonders the File contains." He laughed. "Perhaps an end to capitalism."

"Or even to communism," Strauss said. This time Ruthven frowned. Well, he was a cop, not a diplomat. What did she expect?

Actually, Strauss expected little of this Genesis File. Ever since the Hocq arrived it had been the number one topic of speculation . . . that it would contain the knowledge of a hundred superior races . . . that the scientific and technical breakthroughs would advance the human race by a thousand years. Strauss figured it was just as likely to contain a gold brick carved with the words, "Be good to each other." Why else would the Hocq be so reluctant to give it away?

Stop that. Cynicism increases with fatigue. Strauss's second law.

"As you can imagine, Tim, this news is likely to cause some strain in our already strained relations with California and the Central States." And the rest of the world, for that matter. This was right up there in shock value with the Hitler-Stalin pact. "But if it helps you in making your decisions in the next two days, then you should know about it. Good luck."

"Thank you, Governor. Mr. Bannekker." They hung up.

It would help, all right. Now he hoped nobody got the Genesis File!

CHAPTER 15

Outlaw Territory, Thursday Night

"Harrek, are you ready to leave yet?"

Lisa Marquez tossed the last of her bags into the trunk of the Hurricane and swore. The sun was already behind the hills and Harrek's tent still needed to be taken down—a tricky operation at best and one she had never undertaken in the dark. She had managed to catch a nap following the flight earlier today and had done her packing; now she wanted to get on the road.

As for the Hocq, she didn't honestly know his mood or condition. He had been resting all day, an unusually long time under normal circumstances . . . but then, these were not normal circumstances.

The tent flap opened. "I need your help," Harrek's speaker rasped. "I've already started the depressurization."

"Okay, then, hand me some of your stuff." As Lisa reached for the sleep frame she noticed something odd. "My God, Harrek, what have you got all over your hands?"

The alien continued to hand her pieces of gear. "I believe it is circulatory fluid."

"Blood? Where did you get that? Hold still, please." She bent to examine the greater gloves. No doubt about it: dark crimson smears stained both hands, the left somewhat more than the right. Lisa started to worry. Had he dissected some animal? Or worse?

"During my walk last night I discovered a human corpse. Is it customary in this ethnogeographic Caste to abandon corpses?"

"No, it is not. But are you sure it was human?"

"Yes," Harrek replied. "It fit all the appropriate models."

"Harrek . . . this human body—it was dead when you found it, wasn't it?" She really didn't think he would club a person over the head in the interests of science, but who knew what kind of deadly reflexes a frightened, pre-rashch Hocq might have. He might kill without thinking, if startled. She was thinking of Jeremy Clayton's penchant for showing up without warning.

"This human body had ceased to function an indeterminate time prior to my discovery of it, but the heat loss was considerable. I would estimate that it had been dead for half an Earth rotation, plus or minus one sixth."

Well, if correct, that ruled out Jeremy. But who was it, then? Outlaws? Another stranger? Jeremy's ma or pa? "Well, I wish there was something we could do, but our only alternative is to put some miles between us and this place as soon as we can."

"Agreed." Carrying the compressor, Harrek had emerged completely from the tent. A horrendous odor seemed to emerge with him. Lisa circled the tent warily, knocking down the support struts and shoving them in the trunk of the car. Then, with some effort (considering the smell and the fact that the tent had gotten wet), she rolled the now deflated mylar bag into a bundle, mindful of the need for possible later use.

She took another look at Harrek's hands. "That suit needs a cleaning, but that'll have to wait, too. They're supposed to have some sort of quarters ready for you in Denver, at least."

Lisa felt her heart racing. She stopped to rest for a moment as the alien moved about the farmyard, apparently oblivious to her words or her concerns, clanking around smelling like a robot garbage truck, looking like a mechanical grasshopper seven and a half feet tall. You could help a little, you big goon! And some tough woman you are, Marquez. A couple of days in the woods without a bath, a couple of nights in the back seat of a cruiser, and you come apart at the seams.

Still . . . it was dark now and these hills looked far from friendly. She wanted to be safely in the sky, and soon.

"Harrek," she said again. "Could you please get in the car?"

"Let's go," Ben said. With a wave to Elizabeth in the doorway, he led them away from Hill House and across the old highway.

There were nine of them in all, seven men and two women, dressed for the cold night and, with the exception of a rusty shotgun and an ancient rocket launcher, armed only with axes and picks. Four members of the war party rode two to a horse. The rest went with Ben in the wagon.

"It's going to be tough sneaking up on anyone," Hugh said, noting the flaming torches and the clatter of hooves on the frozen road.

"They'll be quieter once they get going," Ben said. The cold stung his face and he was more tired now than he had been when first insisting on a quick raid. It was a long, unpleasant day, the more so because he did not expect to find anything to justify this effort. The chase would only postpone the moment when he could get to a hot meal and a warm bed. Neil was dead. Let him rest.

Then there was the matter of Jeremy. The boy likely thought his father had spied on him, which was not true . . . not exactly. Ben had only wanted to see for himself the strange goings-on—if any—at the Quiller farm, or at Sun House, for that matter. After all, he had responsibilities for the welfare of others in Arrowsmith.

It was slow going through the hollow, but having driven it only that afternoon Ben was able to avoid the worst holes and ruts. In a few moments they reached and passed the overgrown entrance to the Quiller farm, under the shadow of Willow Ridge. All this fuss, and Ben had yet to take one step onto the Quiller property. Earlier he had merely driven by. The road rose sharply between this place and Sun House, affording the careful if distant observer a clear view of the mysterious farmhouse and environs. But Ben had not reached that point when he found Neil's body lying in plain view in the muddied grass.

"Where exactly are we going?" Hugh asked.

"A little ways yet."

"Mind telling me what you were really doing up here today?"

Ben knew that Hugh would not be satisfied with the same explanation left unquestioned by Dan or Cory. "Oh, you know how the kids have been hanging out at Brandy's a lot lately, and I thought it was time I paid a visit myself." Well, that wasn't the truth, either; responsibilities, again.

Hugh grunted. "Well, it's a good thing you did. Whoever killed that boy could have been long gone before we'd have found him."

"No doubt," Ben said, smiling. "Why don't we pull over right here? This looks like the place."

The pair on the lead horse halted, their torch casting long shadows all around. Ben stopped the wagon to let Hugh out.

Clutching the rocket launcher for dear life, the big man stooped to examine the site in the flickering torch light. "Right about there," Ben said.

Hugh finally set the launcher aside and knelt, taking off his gloves as well. With his bare hand he touched the stained ground where Neil's body had lain. "Lots of blood," he said, "frozen before it dried. Red snow. There's some fresh boot tracks, Ben. Must be yours." He pointed to several spots in an imaginary trail leading back to the road. Looking again, he found a new trail which led back toward Sun House. "Looks like someone killed him over there, then dragged the body down here. What do you think?"

"I didn't take time to think about it. Could be."

"Everything's all flattened out . . ."

"See anything else?"

"Hold that torch steady, will you?" Hugh snapped. He actually got down on his hands and knees. "I see something here . . ."

He straightened up suddenly. "Ben, you said something about funny tracks?"

"Yeah. Find them?"

"I sure have. I've never seen anything like them, either. Come here." He urged his torch-bearer closer. "Must be two inches deep and bigger than my whole hand. Flat in the bottom, too. Doesn't look like any outlaw's boot I can remember."

One of the horses shied. "Sorry," the rider said.

Hugh straightened up. "They could have been put down about the same time as the body. Don't know for sure."

"Where do you think they lead?" Ben said, afraid of the answer.

"Well now, let's see." Silently Hugh circled the site. Eventually he retrieved his launcher and said, "Okay, they come down here from

Sun House, tromp around the body, then cross the road *that* way."
He pointed back the way they had come.

"Back toward the Quiller place," Jolene Horton said.

"Yeah," Ben said. He waited for Hugh to climb aboard. "I guess
it's time we paid a visit."

CHAPTER 16

Arrowsmith, Thursday Night

It was dark when Jeremy finally returned to Hill House. The hours spent fixing the greenhouse window had seemed endless, on a day that had already gone on too long.

He had lost friends before this, but always with some forewarning. They had been ill for days or weeks. One girl had drowned, but she had lived at New House and Jeremy had not known her well.

But he had been with Neil just yesterday morning. He could not believe that the silent, frozen thing lying down at the barn was all that was left of him. Could he have saved him somehow? What if he hadn't spent all that time with Lisa and Harrek?

Heather waited on the front porch. "I was wondering when you'd finally get home," she said, hugging him. "Come inside and get something to eat."

He started to go with her, then hesitated. Something was wrong . . .

"Where's Ben?"

He could have counted half a dozen heartbeats in the time it took her to answer. "He's gone," she said.

"The wagon, too?"

"Yes. Jeremy, wait—"

He pulled away. "Where did he go? To the Quiller place again?"

"They're looking for whoever it was that killed Neil."

"They're not going to find it there."

"Just try to tell Ben that." She moved closer to him again. "Jeremy, there's nothing you can do. You're only hurting yourself. Come inside. Elizabeth and I have been cooking all afternoon. Ben and the others will be back soon, and they'll feel better because they tried. Come on, it's been a sad day."

But Jeremy couldn't stop thinking about Lisa. Suppose she hadn't managed to get away? Ben and the others wouldn't be in any mind to listen to excuses from her . . . much less from Harrek, once they got a look at him.

Suppose Lisa *was* involved in Neil's death? Jeremy had to find out. "How long ago did they leave?" Heather frowned. "Look," he said, "I've got to try, too. Maybe it'll make *me* feel better."

Heather sighed. "Just a few minutes ago."

He buttoned his coat. "How many of them?"

"There were nine altogether. Ben, Hugh, a few others from New House." Her hand was on his shoulder. "Jeremy—"

"Please don't try to stop me."

"I'm not. I just—be careful. Don't surprise them. They've got all kinds of weapons."

"I will. I mean, I won't." He smiled and kissed her. "Tell Elizabeth I'll be a little late for dinner."

Snow had started to swirl through the bare trees when Jeremy reached the crest of Willow Ridge and started down the other side. He had cut right across its spine, hoping to save time. There was still a ghost of a moon in the eastern sky, soon to be obscured by clouds rushing in with a storm. Jeremy wanted it to shine a little longer . . . just a little while longer. Without it, running through these dark woods, he was blind.

The Quiller farm was accessible to wagon only by the driveway off Arrowsmith Road, but there were several cowpaths into the property. Jeremy chose the southern approach; it was quickest to the yard but exited from the trees some distance from the farmhouse itself, which was where Lisa had parked the car and made her camp.

He hoped that by now the Hurricane was on its way to Denver.

He picked his way slowly across the roots which broke the path, stopping twice to ease the ache in his side. Was that torchlight off to his left?

Distracted for an instant, he stumbled and skinned his hands. Ignoring the pain, he got to his feet. If only he could *see*—

The Hurricane hadn't taken off!

Twenty more steps brought him to the relatively smooth ground of the farmyard. He could see it all now: the tricar, still parked, fans running, and nearby . . . four hovering torches.

"Ben!" he shouted. He ran, and fell again, this time getting a mouthful of cold earth. He groaned and wanted to cry.

"Jeremy! Keep away from here!" That sounded like Lisa. Or was it Ben?

He spat, wiped the dirt from his face, and forced himself to stand. Whatever had been going on stopped as he approached. There was Lisa all right, a small weapon in her hand which she aimed at the torchbearers—two of them were Ben and Hugh.

"What are you doing?" Jeremy demanded.

"Keep out of this, Jeremy," Ben said.

Someone else added, "We followed the tracks here. She's got some explaining to do about Neil—"

"She didn't kill anybody," Jeremy said. But he needed time to think. Where was Harrek?

"Listen to this guy," Lisa said calmly. "Save yourselves some real trouble. Jeremy, tell them that the first one who makes a funny move gets turned into a french fry." This was not the same friendly woman with whom Jeremy had spent hours. One look convinced him that she would indeed kill them if she had to. "I'm going to climb into the car and get out of here," she continued. "Make them move back, for their own good."

"You aren't going anywhere, lady—"

"Shut up!" Jeremy shouted. "Do as she says. She can hurt you." He stepped between the two parties.

"Thanks," Lisa whispered. "Harrek!" she called. "Open the front door!"

The door of the Hurricane opened and Harrek could be seen.

The vigilantes gasped and backed away. Lisa edged toward the car, still pointing her weapon. "Harrek, stay where you are—"

"Look at the blood!" Hugh shouted.

Jeremy couldn't believe his eyes. The Hocq's lower hands were smeared with red . . . Neil's blood.

He looked at Lisa. She was shaking her head. "He only *found* him, Jeremy, you've got to believe me—"

A gunshot made him dive to the ground. Harrek seemed to flinch and Lisa threw herself against the car. "You bastards!" she yelled. The weapon in her hand blazed twice.

Two of the torches fell to the ground and went out. Jeremy heard screams and realized that he was too frightened to move. He saw Lisa get safely inside the cruiser, revving the fans to a roar louder than anything he'd ever heard. He tried to crawl away. Ben was shouting to Hugh, who was picking something up off the ground. A long tube.

The Hurricane rose slowly and immediately began to pitch forward.

Hugh's weapon made a whooshing sound and the tricar's front end exploded in a shower of flame. But the car kept rising. Jeremy put his hands over his ears. He screamed for it to stop.

Lisa tried to compensate for the missing lift from the damaged front fans, but the Hurricane wobbled and would not hover. Instead it tilted and swung toward the old barn, touching a corner, spinning in midair, crawling along the wall for a long time before slamming into the building with a horrible, grinding smash. The barn collapsed on top of it.

Suddenly there was total silence. And just as suddenly Jeremy grew aware of moans, voices filled with pain, all around him.

He looked away from the wreckage and saw Ben, Hugh, and Jolene bent over four others who were lying or sitting dazed on the ground. The wounded were trying to warm themselves, but their clothing had disintegrated. Worse yet, they were burned slightly on the chest and hands. No one seemed permanently damaged, however, but they would catch pneumonia if not taken inside immediately. The smell of cooked meat and electrical discharge hung in the air, even though a damp snow had started to fall, collecting in thick clumps.

"I'll get the wagon," Jeremy told Ben, who, stunned, merely nodded.

He didn't have to go far. Two riders who must have been waiting on Arrowsmith Road approached on horseback, bringing the wagon with them. The first rider dismounted. "What was that noise?"

"You've got to get these people back to the house," Jeremy said, taking the reins of the first horse. "They've been burned."

"I can see why!" the second rider was saying.

The old barn, what was left of it, had started to burn. Without releasing the horse, Jeremy moved toward the barn, stooping to retrieve a fallen hatchet. Snow stuck to the blade. He wiped it on his pants.

The fire was not a big one, but the heat could be felt several yards away. "Jeremy, get away from there!" Ben shouted. "That thing might explode!"

He didn't care. He had to do something for Lisa and Harrek—

At that moment someone . . . something cried out. The sound was terrifying and yet sad, more pitiful than the wail of a lost kitten and about ten times as loud. It had to be Harrek.

Fallen flaming boards were being pushed aside in the wreckage. Harrek's bubbled head appeared for a moment, slipped back, then reappeared. This time it was followed by his lesser hand, which clawed at the surrounding clutter with impossible speed and strength.

The horse was nervous. "Wait," Jeremy muttered, soothing it. He quickly found a short piece of wood and with the blunt of the hatchet pounded it into the ground like a stake. He tied the horse, then plunged into the ruined barn.

Harrek cried again.

The Hocq had crawled halfway out of the wrecked aftersection of the Hurricane. It took three blows with the hatchet to free him, and the alien immediately stood up, pushing with his greater arms and looking for all the world like a tall tree righting itself in a storm solely by using its roots. Jeremy grabbed one of the stained hands and tugged Harrek out of the flames.

He left the alien with the horse, which was not grateful for the company, and returned to the barn. The fire was dying now—a good thing, since the wind was rising. Jeremy could see that the front of the Hurricane had been crushed. As he watched helplessly, there was a series of small explosions from the engine section that brought the rest of the barn down.

He was too numb to react, too cold. He had known Lisa was dead the moment the cruiser smashed into the wall. Presently he turned away, the hatchet firmly in his hand.

Ben and Hugh were waiting for him well out of Harrek's reach. The Hocq had collapsed into a grotesque squat; his suit was torn and blackened and snow was gathering on it. "Stay where you are," Jeremy ordered the two men. He moved closer to Harrek. "Can you climb up on the horse?"

The alien didn't answer but did get slowly to his feet. The horse tugged at her stake. Jeremy grabbed the reins to calm her. "It's all right," he said, "just hold still." He kept glancing over at Ben and Hugh, making sure they could see the hatchet. He blinked to clear his vision. Melting snow.

"Just what do you think you're doing?" Ben said.

"I'm taking him out of here," Jeremy replied. He didn't have the energy to shout anymore. He didn't much care if they heard him or not.

"You don't know what you're doing, son. You don't even know what that thing is."

Harrek had managed to get up on the horse. His long legs almost touched the ground. Both pairs of arms were wrapped around the animal's neck. "We're going now," Jeremy told Harrek. "Hang on."

He led them straight toward Ben, who slowly stepped aside. "Don't," Ben said.

Jeremy looked at him. "She didn't do anything to Neil, Ben, and neither did Harrek. And they could have *killed* all of you, if they wanted. You know that, too."

He passed the wagon full of the injured. "You better get going," he told them. "You'll freeze out here." Snow continued to fall.

When they reached Arrowsmith Road, Jeremy took a right, the turn that would lead him away from Hill House.

Rob Prescott hurried outside the house in a T-shirt when he heard the not-so-distant explosion. Stagger, who had been standing watch down at the end of the driveway, met him immediately, pointing his rifle at the surrounding hills as if he expected to see a fleet of CSA choppers.

"You heard it, too, huh?"

"Hell yes," Prescott said. "I even *felt* it." He waved Canfield and the others back into the house.

"What do you think it was?"

"You've got me there. It didn't really sound like a bomb, but you can't tell when the weather gets like this. Funny things happen to sounds." Or to ears. Prescott wished he'd grabbed his coat; snow was getting down his shirt.

Stagger had relaxed enough to lower his rifle. "How much longer are we gonna hide out here, anyway?"

"Until the radio tells me the Third Division has gone home to beddy-bye," he snapped. He was tired and irritable. They'd been shut up in this crummy place for going on two days—not cooking for fear of drawing choppers, not moving, trying to make a badly wounded man comfortable with just a first-aid kit, standing cold watches on all the approaches, jumping at the slightest sounds. And there was no relief in sight. Four times a day Prescott crawled up the hill to listen to reports from CSA patrols and search aircraft, and all he got was no news—which was bad news. *Something* was happening out there . . . but he didn't know what.

Of course, Third Division or not, sooner or later they would have to make a run for it. They had found nothing in the way of edible food in the house or in the weird little lean-to, and their own stock of emergency rations had been low to begin with. More important, their Chicago fence would be gone if they didn't make rendezvous by the middle of next week. If they couldn't make the deal, they might as well be dead. You couldn't eat microchips or metal.

"What are we gonna do if it keeps snowing like this?" Stagger asked.

"Build a snowman," Prescott said. "I don't *know*, Stagger. Why don't you get back to your post?" Stagger pouted. "I'll walk you, okay?

"Look, if there's a major storm we might be able to slip through. We know these back roads and it's a lot easier for us to move a couple of jeeps around than it is for them to move a platoon of soldiers." He did wish they could rig the big comm unit to pick up satellite weather . . . their regular dish had been on the carrier.

"Why don't we just shoot our way out? Jump some of these blue bastards and take their uniforms? They've gotta be spread pretty thin —we could break through and be gone before they know it."

They stopped and huddled under the trees where the driveway met Arrowsmith Road. They kept their voices low. There was still that boom! to explain . . .

"You keep forgetting, Stagger, that we aren't just dealing with a couple of weekend warriors and some jeeps here. This is big casino; those guys out there are pros. One of their choppers can cover the ground from here to the Mississippi in less time than you took crapping this morning."

Stagger held up his hand. "I hear something."

Prescott did, too. Hoofbeats and nothing else, not far away.

"We'll have to take them," he said.

Without being told, Stagger slapped a pistol and a flashlight into Prescott's open hands, then moved off down the road in the opposite direction. Prescott flattened himself in the snow, which was already an inch deep.

He could see the intruder now . . . two men, one walking, leading a horse, the other riding. The rider looked damned tall. They passed, making no sound other than muffled footfalls. Prescott counted to three, then stepped into the road behind them. "Hold it, neighbor," he said pleasantly.

The walking figure froze, then turned. As he did Prescott thumbed the switch on his light.

"Who are you?" the walker said, trying to calm his horse and shade his eyes at the same time.

Stagger was on the road beyond them, giggling. "Chamber of Commerce," he said.

Prescott swept the light up to the rider, the second of his new prisoners—

Jesus Christ!

CHAPTER 17

West Union, Central States, Friday Morning

In this Year of Our Lord 2038, almost halfway through the twenty-first century, it should not take eight hours to travel seventy-odd miles by land, thought Tim Strauss as he prepared to leave his room at the decidedly unsumptuous Bailor Hotel in West Union. Nevertheless, eight hours had elapsed from the moment he supervised the loading of Boroz into a CSA truck until they pulled into town late last night. Their route had taken them from Dubuque past Independence, then toward Waterloo, once reports from the quarantine indicated that the Hurricane had come to rest near the town of West Union. Strauss had then spent an additional three hours getting Boroz safely put to bed, a procedure which required a considerable amount of negotiation with the hotel's manager, who could not be convinced that the Hocq's portable pressure suit and tent would not permanently damage or contaminate his rooms. Perhaps there was a sort of universal standard of decrepitude barrier . . . one more bit of damage or wear and the Bailor's rooms would reach it. Fortunately the local militia commander, a Colonel Lippert, got the man to see reason. The nature of the disagreement ensured, however, that Strauss's room would be the size of a closet. He wasn't going to worry about that now; he hadn't spent nearly enough time in it to begin to feel cramped.

He left the room, zipping his new CSA fatigue jacket against the chill of the Bailor's drafty halls. The hotel wasn't much these days—no surprise, given the lack of a tourist trade in this part of the country—but Strauss seriously doubted that the crumbling, century-old, three-story monstrosity had ever made the travel guides. But it was better, at least on paper, than camping out in the snow . . .

He knocked on the door of the big room immediately down the hall, waking up Shapiro, who answered the door with the face of a man with a terminal illness. "Good morning," Strauss said cheerfully. "How's our star boarder? No pun intended."

Shapiro moved aside to let Strauss into the room. More than half was taken up by an olive-drab pressure tent inside which Boroz presumably rested. "Haven't heard a peep out of her. How much are the Hocq supposed to rest, anyway?"

"Six hours out of thirty. About what you're getting."

"That's twice what I'm getting." Shapiro yawned. "What time is it?"

"Six-fifteen. Lippert told me last night that he expected to have the whole quarantine area mapped, surveyed and analyzed by seven."

"Then what?" Shapiro went into the bathroom, carrying his electric razor. Strauss went with him.

"Well, first of all, a good analysis of the surveys should tell us where the Hurricane is stashed, even if it's inside a building. They were supposed to be doing enhancements last night. Once we've got Marquez's location pinned down, and assuming that the perimeter is secure, we move in, taking the Ambassador along, and get Harrek and Marquez back. With a little luck we might be back in Austin in time for the game with TCU tomorrow."

Strauss sensed that Shapiro felt more than a little uncomfortable sharing the bathroom. The young man was obviously not of the Lyndon Johnson school of politics. Strauss headed for the door. "You'll take care of the Ambassador's wakeup call," he whispered.

The only sounds in the room were the wump-wump of a compressor inside the tent—which must have made Shapiro's attempts at sleep totally futile—and the buzz of a razor. "I'll get her up in fifteen minutes," Shapiro said, "if she's not already awake."

"Good. Lippert's jeep will be out front at seven. Boroz might as well be there when we are."

"Tim?"

"Yes?"

"Ah . . . have you ever had to wake up one of these folks? What am I supposed to do?"

"Well," Strauss said, amused, "you could go in there and tickle her. The air pressure is slightly higher and the oxygen content slightly lower—you'd survive *that*. But I suspect that the Hocq are a bit grouchy when awakened. Take the safe way. Bang on a pot or a tin can and stand back!"

He went downstairs, through the empty lobby—there wasn't a clerk on duty at the desk—and crossed the slushy street to a café named the Sweet Pea. Strauss thanked God he had had the foresight to convert to local currency before getting on the plane Tuesday night. After that midnight debate with the Bailor's manager he didn't even want to think about the problems he would have getting a cup of coffee in a diner in the rustic depths of the Central States at six in the morning using a Texan credit card. He found a booth near the window and slid in.

There was one waitress, an elderly woman in an old-fashioned pink pantsuit. Four men in Martin Farms uniforms sat at the counter. In one of the other booths Strauss noted a trio of CSA militia men in fatigues; in a second was a more unusual group—two men and two women wearing the latest from the Gold Coast or Rodeo Drive. One of the women looked Hispanic. Interesting . . .

"Morning," the waitress said. "Coffee?"

"Yes, please." Strauss accepted a menu. It wasn't lengthy. "I'll have the number four, only I'd like a double order of pancakes and toast."

Strauss unzipped his jacket and sat back. Normally he had little time for private meals when traveling on Ranger business, which was a shame. He didn't much care for "working" lunches.

"Captain Strauss?"

He looked from the window as a woman slid into his booth. It was the Hispanic member of the trendy quartet. "Is there something I can do for you?"

"Sorry to disturb you," she said, not sounding sorry at all. "I'm Teri Pedroza, CBS News."

He didn't permit his expression to change but his otherwise unnoticeable accent grew more prominent. "My, you folks sure do get around."

"So do you, it seems. You know that I'm with the Hocq pool."

"I recall some mention of that, yes." His coffee arrived. He did not order for Pedroza. "I'm not giving any interviews at the moment."

"I wouldn't think so," she said coolly. "I understand that you've got Dr. Marquez and the fugitive Hocq located and will be moving in on them this morning."

"I would categorize that statement as quite premature."

"Come on, Captain. Those CSA recon photos found the Hurricane, according to my sources."

Strauss hated having the press get to his data before he did. Pedroza was good. She'd actually given information to Strauss. According to the code, he was bound to give something in return. He drank some coffee. "I think that's an exaggeration," he said finally. "You know how ambiguous even the best low-level recon material can be in cases like this."

"But you *are* going out to the quarantine area in the next few hours."

"I'm sure you don't need a word from me to confirm or deny that." The waitress had arrived with his breakfast. Real bacon! Just the aroma was enough to make him feel better. "Would you care to join me?" he asked Pedroza. "On CBS, of course."

"I thought you'd never ask. Thank you." She ordered coffee and set a tiny chip recorder on the table. "You don't mind, do you? If nothing else, it'll help with my expense account."

"Of course. It isn't every day that I'm interviewed by a famous reporter from California."

"Considering how popular the press is in Texas, I'm surprised you've been interviewed at all."

"Oh, we still have a few 'objective observers' around. Although they are on the endangered-species list. Where are you from, Ms. Pedroza?"

"Santa Ana," she said.

"That's near Anaheim, isn't it?"

"Right next door."

"You know, I do believe Lisa Marquez was born in Anaheim before moving to Texas."

"So I hear." Pedroza fiddled with her recorder, which had seemed to be functioning perfectly.

"Well then, what exactly can I do for you, for CBS and for the free press everywhere? Aside from giving you answers I don't have."

"Okay, let's forget about today's activities for the moment. Has anyone figured out why a member of the Governor's inner circle of advisers would simply—"

"Excuse me, but I would not characterize Lisa Marquez as a close adviser to the Governor. She's a staff employee, yes, but not a member of any 'inner circle,' if indeed there is such a thing."

She frowned. "Then you've gone to all this trouble for a runaway secretary?"

He smiled at the deliberate misstatement. "I believe the 'fuss,' as you put it, is over a member of an extraterrestrial species who has, for reasons of his own, absented himself from his fellow travelers. This rescue operation is being jointly managed by several governments, by the way. Texas is merely a junior member. We're here, in fact, precisely because we're as curious as you are why Lisa Marquez is involved."

"How did she get hooked up with the alien in the first place?"

"You tell me." His voice had gotten loud enough to draw looks from the other diners, including Pedroza's fellow reporters. One of them, a small black man, got up and approached their booth. Not wanting to be double-teamed, Strauss threw his napkin on the table and got up. "You should probably direct these questions to Colonel Lippert. He's the local authority. See you later."

Only when he got halfway across the street did Strauss realize that he had eaten just two bites of his breakfast.

Contrary to Shapiro's assumption, Boroz had not slept the previous night. She had not slept, in fact, during this entire Earth week, not since learning of her troublesome brother's treachery and disappearance. Such abstinence, though unusual, was not completely unprecedented. Boroz had remained awake for a comparable period during her own rashch—the result of which, ironically, was treacherous Harrek—and during the final preparations for this long voyage across the interstellar night. During the latter she had come close to a breakdown . . . from frustration at her assigned "mission," from despair, from fear. She had been ready to renounce her First rather than devote so many years of her life to this silly idea of going to other worlds. Even now she would meditate upon the difficulties of communication and survival on strange planets, upon the small likelihood of any real exchange between the people of Earth and her People, upon a thousand other slights and annoyances.

But the First of the First Caste had crossed the Beggar's Plain millennia ago for reasons as good or bad. Thus, when the stars spoke of exploration, wandering, teaching—not forgetting that the knowledge to explore, to wander and to teach had come from the stars— cross the desert of night she would.

It was only the voices buried deep within her, the collected wisdom and experiences of a string of conjugant sisters stretching back to the First of the First, that brought Boroz to this door. The price was high: she would certainly lose her rare second rashch; when she returned from this mission she would be too old. Was that why she was so furious that now she faced doors chosen by Harrek?

"Excellency?" The more subservient of her two Earth attendants cowered near the tent's opening. She should see him fluttering nervously about like some small desert creature fit only for a meal. "Excuse me, but I've been told we will be leaving shortly . . ."

Boroz sealed her protective garment and thrust herself out of the tiny tent, startling the Earth man, as she intended. "When will we leave, precisely? I am familiar with your units."

"In ten minutes," the man said. "Ah . . . is there anything I can do for you?"

"No," she said. Proper usage suggested an expression of gratitude for the Earth man's offer of assistance, but Boroz suspected it would be more useful to forego it for now. "Where is the vehicle?"

"It will be in front of the hotel."

Boroz arranged her limbs and performed a systems check on the suit. All was in order, within and without—a pleasant surprise. The Earth people never ceased to astound her with their mechanical skills. If only those skills were transferrable—trade bait—the Genesis material could be licensed and Boroz could return to Ashentar.

First, however, Harrek must be dealt with.

"Lead me to the vehicle," Boroz said.

CHAPTER 18

Outlaw Territory, Friday Morning

"Wake up, kid."

Jeremy flinched at the sudden voice and blinked, turning his head away from the blinding light that shone in his face. It was difficult to move at all: his hands were bound behind his back and he'd slept on his left arm all night. It felt as if a horse had stepped on it.

"Come *on.*" Someone hauled him to his feet.

"Okay! I'm up," he said. The hands released him and went to work on his bonds. He had spent the night on the floor of the Sun House barn, kept company by two battered jeeps, a three-axle wagon, and two restless horses. It was far less comfortable than it had been earlier in the week, but then, he had been much younger then. Or so it seemed. He rubbed his wrists as his two captors pushed him outside.

The sun was newly up, enough so that the whole of Sun House and environs was visible. Jeremy was surprised that it still looked the same. Where was Brandy Kramer?

His captors led him to the front door, which had been broken in. The house looked torn up, but Jeremy wasn't prepared to blame that entirely on the outlaws; Brandy wasn't terribly neat, either. That was one of the reasons she lived alone. A pair of fine old tables had been upended and shoved against the front windows. Sleeping bags were scattered on the floor, and here and there were piles of empty food containers. Jeremy judged that there were at least half a dozen out-laws holed up here: he had seen two men last night and two more just now, and counted five sleeping bags.

"Wait right here," one of his captors told him, "and don't move."

It was unnecessary to add that because the second outlaw remained in the doorway directly behind him.

A third man entered the living room. Jeremy recognized him as one of the pair that had captured him last night. "You want something to eat?"

He was starving; he nodded. "Rickie," the outlaw said, "get our guest something. I'm going to have a little chat with him." Looking unhappy, the first outlaw went out to the kitchen. "Sit down, sit down. What's your name?"

"Jeremy Clayton."

"Jeremy. Well, I'm Rob Prescott, and on behalf of the rest of the Pirates, I want to tell you that we're really sorry for the inconvenience." He grinned. "We're a little nervous about strangers at the moment. Comes with the job, I guess."

"I thought you guys were the strangers around here."

Prescott laughed. He was not bigger than Jeremy and did not, in fact, look as if he wouldn't fit right in, in Arrowsmith. His hands and face were darkened by the sun, and his hair, what was left of it, had been tied into a long ponytail that fell down his back. "That's very true. You have a good point. You must live around here."

"Up the road a couple of miles." Jeremy was too tired, hungry, and sore to lie.

Prescott got serious all of a sudden. "Well, you may be from these parts, Jeremy, but it's for damn sure your traveling companion isn't. What's the deal? What's the connection?"

He hadn't even thought about Harrek! "Is he all right?"

"How the hell should I know? About all I can tell you is that he wasn't stiff last time I looked. Although I don't even know if something like that would go cold when it died."

Rickie returned from the kitchen with a dirty jar of apple juice and a bowl of what appeared to be oatmeal. He took a wooden spoon— one of Brandy's wooden spoons—out of his shirt pocket and handed it to Jeremy, then sat in the corner and watched.

"You still haven't answered my question, Jeremy."

His mouth was full. "I don't know why he's here," he said. "There was an accident. I'm helping him out. That's all there is to it."

"That's all, huh. I suppose he was just taking a vacation out here, then. Canfield? What do you guys think? You're always full of ideas."

The outlaw guarding the front door spoke. "It might explain why the CSA has all those troops out. We know they aren't after us—"

"—though they'd take us, too, if they could," Rickie added from his corner.

"No one knows what the Hocq want or what they can give. That's been the big problem for the Texans or whoever's had to deal with them," Canfield said. "Everyone's scared of them. That's what the news says."

"I can see why," Prescott said. "Be glad you didn't meet up with him the way I did." The outlaw chief got out of his chair and paced around the room. "Hey, Jeremy, mind telling me where you were taking this guy?"

Where indeed? "To town. West Union. I guess I thought I could get help for him there."

"That'd be a first," Rickie said contemptuously.

Prescott was silent for a moment, then said, "Come with me."

Jeremy set aside his breakfast and followed the outlaw to an adjoining room. There he found Harrek, his protective suit torn, sprawled across two mattresses on the floor.

"He let us lead him in here last night," Prescott said. "I tell you, it's kind of hard to believe that this guy traveled all the way across the galaxy to wind up dead on some farm."

"I don't think he planned it that way." Jeremy could hear the faint hiss of Harrek's breathing—he took that as a good sign. "What are you going to do with us?"

Prescott's expression never changed. "I should really kill both of you and toss your bodies into the woods. I've got a lot of ground to cover and the one thing I don't need is prisoners. But—"

The outlaw's casual discussion of his potential murder didn't upset Jeremy, even though he had realized since last night that these were Neil's killers. As far as he was concerned, his own life had effectively ended sometime Wednesday. Everything since had been beyond his control or comprehension . . . a dream that had gone on too long.

"But," Jeremy repeated.

"But this guy is important to the CSA and a lot of other people, too. I assume they want him back at nearly any price." He grinned again. "Maybe even amnesty for some poor outlaws. Why don't you get him ready to travel? I think we might be moving out this morning. But be careful, kid. If he dies, I've got no reason to keep you alive."

CHAPTER 19

West Union, CSA, Friday Morning

One by one, four heavy CSA choppers roared up from the landing zone with a spray of snow and mud. In the tail-end craft Strauss gripped the restraining bar for dear life, in spite of the fact that he was securely belted in. He was the passenger closest to the open door, and when the chopper tilted to one side to make the wide turn into the hills, he had a clear view of the roofs of West Union.

Boroz sat next to him, much like a grizzly bear wedged into a back seat. Shapiro was on the other side. Colonel Lippert and an aide faced them, having climbed aboard at the last moment. Liftoff time was actually nine o'clock, two hours late. Strauss had been unable to find Colonel Lippert in that time.

"Colonel," Strauss shouted. "I have heard that you've got a hard location on the Hurricane."

Lippert was a beefy, pale-faced man with a pencil-thin mustache. He reminded Strauss of a mildly crooked Panhandle sheriff he'd once busted. "Not quite, sir. I don't know where you could have heard anything like that. We have a tentative hot spot—"

"Infrared source?"

"Yes, sir. We've got infrared data from a couple of sorties over the quarantine area early this morning, about two. One high altitude, one low. The trouble is—" The colonel's throat was beginning to hurt from all the shouting. He calmly reached into space and slid the chopper door shut. "Trouble is," he continued, "there are at least *three* hot spots on the low-level product."

"Is that unusual?"

"Yes, sir, it sure is. I mean, we know that there are habitations in the quarantine area—dropouts, most of them—and the scans do show these hot spots. These other three have completely different signatures. Three different IR sources where there should be just one."

"So either you've incorrectly identified the motor-vehicle signatures, or Lisa Marquez has company up there." It was the second possibility that worried him the most. He was convinced that the woman had disappeared inside the quarantine area; a mistake in location would only mean a delay . . . but if she had accomplices—armed assistance—it could get nasty.

Lippert, however, looked smug. "I doubt that we would mistake a campfire or a heated building for a vehicle. You wouldn't make a mistake like that just looking at them on the street—"

"I'm familiar with most surveillance methods, Colonel."

Shapiro stirred from his coma and spoke up. "What about a visual search?"

"That was the first thing we tried, of course. We didn't find the Hurricane—but we really didn't expect to. There's just too much ground cover. You've got to know this area to realize that, I suppose. It's not much this side of wilderness. There are some good-sized fields that have survived over the years, but once you get into that hilly region you can't see anything from the air. Not even most of the houses. We even came across an outlaw band that must have gotten caught up in the quarantine by accident."

"What about outlaws?" Strauss asked, annoyed. This was the first mention of any outlaws.

"The report I have is that they were wiped out. We caught 'em on a bridge, and it was an armored gunship that found 'em, too." He shrugged, as if to say, poor bastards.

"I assume there's confirmation of that. Bodies, perhaps."

"Ah, no, sir," Lippert said. "We're going by the crew's mission report. A ground patrol should be reconnoitering that site sometime this morning, however—"

"Then it's possible that one or two or all three of your so-called hot spots might very well belong to some outlaws and not to our missing tricar."

"Anything's possible, of course, but I don't think—"

Strauss rarely lost his temper, but he was close now, his anger fueled by Lippert's bland, misplaced confidence and his own lack of sleep. "Damn it, Colonel, I won't have this operation screwed up by your hunches and assumptions! You've dragged the Ambassador and me into a potentially dangerous situation with no hard evidence that the people we're looking for are even here! What are you going to do? Land us on top of one of your little hot spots? Suppose we land on some hostile outlaws instead? Are you telling me that you've risked the lives of your men, of those press people, and the *ambassador of an alien race* on some *hunch?*"

Strauss kept his voice low. He didn't mind chewing the fool out in front of Shapiro, and especially not in front of Boroz, who seemed to take perverse joy in the spectacle of Earth men humiliating each other—but embarrassing Lippert in front of his own aide and en-listed men would eventually cause him more problems than would a little midmorning firefight. He tried to smooth things over. "Look, I'm sure that there's been a lot of pressure on you from high places to wrap this thing up as quickly as possible"—Strauss neglected to acknowledge that he was the source of much of the pressure—"but I'll be happy to take the responsibility for delaying our first move long enough to make sure it's safe. How far away are your ground troops?"

"I could have a company at the target point in less than an hour."

"Excellent. Let's set down on the nearest safe high ground. We can rendezvous with the ground forces there, and check out all three of these hot spots, if necessary, at that time. By the way, how far apart are these things?"

"Two of them are paired just a few yards apart, and the pair is located about two miles north-northwest of the third spot."

"And where in relation to them is the nearest safe landing zone?"

He waited while Lippert's aide worked an electronic mapboard. Lippert screwed up his face, then said, "About two more miles south of that solo hot spot. The rest of this is all hills. I had to try to move four choppers and an infantry company in and out of that stuff."

"Looks to me, Colonel, like it's possible for us to check out all three potential hiding places—using ground support—and still be back at the Bailor for lunch."

"We might just do that, yes, sir. Excuse me." Lippert and the aide went forward to the pilot's cabin and comm unit.

Strauss turned to Boroz. "I apologize for the added excitement, Excellency. It was your safety I was thinking of."

The Hocq wheezed, "An apology is not required. I found it quite entertaining."

Strauss suppressed a smile and looked out the window. Below them a river passed, followed by ravines, hills choked with trees, the miles-wide scar of some old tornado passage. At least Lippert had been right about the uselessness of aerial reconnaissance. The tops of the trees still glistened with snow partially melted from last night's fall. But Strauss suspected that this day had gotten as bright and as warm as it would ever get.

"Tim," Shapiro said, "take a look over here. You won't believe it."

He leaned forward for a view out the other side of the chopper. Shapiro said, "Good God, isn't that an old wind generator out there?"

The sounds of a great commotion up the hill carried all the way down to New House. Dan Aucheron went to an upstairs window and looked out, alarmed at the distant shouts and the strange womp-womping noise.

Helicopters were circling over Hill House. The outsider invasion had finally arrived.

"Hugh! Where are you?" Dan took the stairs as fast as he could. Somehow this new menace was not unexpected, not after the strange events of the day before, and certainly after the whispers he'd heard about what happened last night. First they'd found that poor dead boy, and then Ben and the others going off on that raid, returning scared and dirty and full of wild stories. Hugh had told somebody that they'd found the killer, and that young Jeremy had run off with him! You always had to wait a day or two to get the full story—he hadn't talked to Hugh yet himself, or to Ben either.

A crowd had gathered outside New House, all of them—maybe a dozen in all—staring up toward the Hill.

Dan spied Hugh near the front of the throng. "Is that the kind of machine you folks saw last night?"

Hugh seemed surprised at being addressed. "Doesn't look like it," he said, wiping his hand across his mouth. "But I can't really say for sure. It was pretty dark."

"Hmph. You've lived all your *life* in the dark, son. Get me that ax over there. Now—" Dan turned to face the crowd. They were frightened, that was plain. Each looked to a neighbor for support, then back to the Hill, where those infernal machines continued to circle and roar. No one said a word. Dan believed that had he been a few years younger he could have smelled the fear.

"They're landing," Cissy Funderburk said.

It was true. The flying machines hovered briefly, then settled one by one to the ground. It was hard to see more than that from this distance.

"I'm going up there," Dan announced. "If anyone feels like coming with me, I'd be happy for the company. Of course, somebody's got to stay here and keep an eye on things." Let the rest hold onto some of their pride. They might need it one day.

No one volunteered. In a way he didn't blame them. It was very likely that they didn't see this as a dangerous situation—just old Dan getting worked up over nothing. After all, most of them had been children at best during the war years; certainly none remembered the early days, when tourists and townspeople came to New House like it was some sort of zoo, tromping through the gardens, taking pictures, stealing. The war years had been the worst, however. Even Highway 56 had been choked with the cars of people trying to escape the plague weapons. And once the first exodus passed they had had to be so careful about any strangers. Dan had killed one woman himself, over toward Sun House, to keep her from possibly bringing some kind of disease into the community. That nobody remembered those incidents was a testament to Dan. He'd worked hard to keep it quiet.

"There's a bunch of people running around up there." One of the women had gone to an upstairs window in the house for a better view.

"It might be best for all of you to stay inside till I get back," Dan said. He hefted the ax, then headed toward the old path which, it occurred to him, was not quite as old as he was.

He slipped past the north wall of the greenhouse—now secured against the weather, he noted with approval—past a frightened Cory, who stood there with hoe in hand looking about as strong and resourceful as that fifty-year-old windmill farther up the Hill. Dan was afraid that if he said hello the boy would run.

Something stirred inside him, a feeling of excitement reminiscent of his first love. A wind blew at his back like a gentle push, urging him on against the invaders.

He headed off the path before reaching the Hill House compound. Cover here was sparse, nothing more than a low vine-covered fence which marked the property line of the old Pratt farm, cutting at right angles from the northeast to southwest across the path. Dan followed the fence to his left, down the hill, so as to keep the barn between him and the invaders. Presently he found a break in the fence, a place where runoff had dug a trench in the ground beneath it. He knelt, shoved the ax through, then squeezed under the boards himself.

He had to catch his breath for a moment, and think.

The womp-womping noise had stopped, replaced by the sounds of voices that carried clear across the compound. The information told him little, however. He crawled forward slowly, on his hands and knees, keeping to the fence line. Beneath the covering of dead grass the ground was soft in places, and these soft spots were usually muddy. Dan dirtied his knees and elbows but kept moving: a little earth couldn't keep him from helping Ben and the others.

He changed direction as the ground began to flatten out, heading away from the fence now and straight across the compound toward the south side of the barn. He chanced a quick look at the invaders—

The helicopters had set down at the absolute crest of the ridge, just above the house in the field dominated by the old windmill. A small number of people—soldiers!—were fanning out toward the highway in a ragged line. Another group was conferring in the midst of flapping paper and scattered electronic equipment, while a third marched toward the house itself. Dan noted that the soldiers carried their rifles on their backs and seemed to be relaxed, not expecting trouble. Further confirmation came from their voices, which he could hear clearly now. They were laughing and talking as if on a picnic.

Where were Ben and the rest? He couldn't see anyone but invaders from here. He would simply have to find a better vantage point.

Carefully he got to a crouch and started to run toward the barn. There was a pronounced ache in his side and another one in the middle of his back by now, due to the unaccustomed exercise. He was even unsteady on his feet and helpless to change it. When at last he reached the safety of the barn he had to rest for quite a while. The ax had gotten noticeably heavier, and the wind, now blowing in his face, took his breath away.

He knew his options were limited. An attack on the helicopters, though it appealed to his reborn sense of adventure, was impossible, even if he had all of Arrowsmith with him. These outsiders possessed weapons more dangerous than those of any outlaw, and Dan had seen what outlaw automatic weapons could do. But he had to find Ben and Elizabeth or any of the house residents, to help them get away if he could, or at least let them know the rest of the community was doing what it could do.

Get up in the barn, he thought, up in the loft where you can see . . .

Steadying himself with one hand pressed against the ancient stone foundation, Dan moved from the downhill side of the barn around to the west. There he had a brief glance directly at Hill House, which looked undisturbed. He moved quickly now, found the latch of the sliding door, and pushed it open far enough to slide through. It creaked madly.

Had he been too noisy? With a speed he had not known for twenty years, he scurried away into the darkness, then froze. He hadn't attempted to close the door behind him, fearful of setting off more unnecessary creakings.

He let his eyes adjust. There was a ladder high up in the north wall, accessible only from the left—and the loft was reachable only by a ladder. Where was it? He hadn't been in here in years. Yes, against the wall in the near corner.

He picked his way across the floorboards, between rows of fragrant hay bales. He was glad he'd managed to get into the building on the upper level. There were animals down below that surely would have raised a ruckus at his sudden appearance. His hands touched the ladder, and he noted that he was now able to see, except for the droplet of sweat that blurred the right lens of his glasses. He would rest once more before beginning the climb—

He heard a thump nearby.

"Is that you, Ben?" a woman's voice said.

"*Shut up!*" he hissed. "It's Dan." Who the hell was stupid enough to make so much noise?

"Why, Dan! I haven't seen you forever."

Not ten feet away Brandy Kramer stood up, brushing herself off, her voice loud enough to be heard in West Union.

"Can't you quiet down a little, Brandy? We've got trouble out there."

She winked, and after a bit of thought, apparently decided to make the effort. "Oh I know *that*. I'm not stupid, Dan. I saw those machines."

"What are you doing here? Where are the rest?"

She came closer, smelling of the woods, her head turning every which way but toward him. "I haven't been able to get home for three days," she said. "People at my place. I didn't invite them, no way. Did you?"

"No, Brandy, I didn't send anybody to your place. I wouldn't do that." She hadn't changed. He became aware of a stirring behind Brandy. It was a younger woman bundled in a tattered blanket, propped up against the bales. She looked asleep or unconscious— certainly hurt. "Who's this?"

"Oh, her. You know, Dan, it's funny. I found her at the other farm, you know, the old one where no one lives. There was a fire there, I think. I went over there looking for a place to stay out of the snow—"

You could spend your remaining years waiting for Brandy to give you an answer. "Brandy! Who *is* she? Did she tell you her name?"

"She said her name was Lisa something. Lisa—isn't that a pretty name?"

"Did you see the choppers?" Stagger yelled, running up to the house.

"I heard them," Prescott said. "I was inside. It sounded like they were circling." There was nothing in the sky now, but only moments ago several roaring machines had buzzed the place.

"Yeah, I saw them make a loop," Stagger said. "They were pretty high up, though."

"Who knows if they were looking for us, or just screwing around." Prescott continued to search the sky. It was midmorning, though the cloudiness made it hard to tell. "Where did they come from?"

"Northwest, it looked like." Stagger was still trying to catch his breath.

"How many?"

"I saw four. Come to think of it, they might have landed south of here."

"Dammit." That settled it. They were still a day from their planned move, but with CSA choppers overhead and landing in the neighborhood it was obvious they couldn't wait any longer. "How much time will it take to get the jeeps and the wagon on the road?"

Stagger shrugged. "Not more than half an hour, if that's what you want. How's Johnston?"

"Stable." As far as the wounded man was concerned it probably didn't make much difference what Prescott decided. If they tried to run for it, Johnston was dead.

"What about . . . the other two?" Stagger's usual sneer was gone, replaced by a genuine curiosity.

"The kid won't be a problem. The Man from Mars—well, I just don't know. He might be worse off than Johnston."

"We could leave them."

"We need them." Prescott grinned. "Cheer up. You wanted to blow away a bunch of bluejackets. Today could be your big chance. Tell Canfield I want to see him. And get the wheels loaded."

As Stagger ran off, Prescott stood and took in his surroundings. Was this the day it all caught up with him? He felt the need of a time-out, a stay of sentence. He was worried because until now, no matter what the trouble, he had always been able to see beyond it. Not today. What the hell. Time to look in on Johnston.

He grabbed his gear and went into the back room. "How're you doing?"

Johnston didn't even try to smile. "Hanging in there. I've been better." The poor son of a bitch was pale and, with good reason, scared to death. He'd lost a lot of blood when the fragments ripped into his body, and had suffered internal injuries and a broken leg when he was thrown from the carrier. He was lucky to be alive but that luck had just about run out. He needed a doctor and a hospital.

"We've got you pretty doped up."

Now he tried to smile. "Don't get me addicted."

"No problem."

"Sorry I screwed up."

"You didn't screw up. If anybody screwed up, it was me. I took us over the bridge." He sat on the edge of the bed and took Johnston's pulse. It was present; nothing more could be said about it. "Hey, we're going to have to clear out of here this morning. Think you're up to a ride?"

Johnston took a long, pain-wracked breath. "What choice do I have?"

"You could stay right here. Maybe Stagger could stay with you until we're clear." Stagger would like that. All he'd want is a pair of autorifles and five hundred rounds of ammo. "We could send a medic in a few hours. But we've got to bust out of here now."

"I . . . I don't want you to leave me here, okay? They're hanging guys like us. Besides, the food here is terrible."

Prescott had to laugh. He'd always liked Johnston. "Okay, you're coming with us." He liked the man's choice, too. It was better to die with friends than alone in a strange place. Remember that. "I'll come get you when we're ready. Rest up now." He squeezed Johnston's hand.

Johnston tried to raise himself to a sitting position. "I'll be okay."

"I know you will."

The alien was Prescott's next problem.

He found the creature half out of its bed, bent forward, with the kid working on its chest pack. Prescott hadn't really looked at the alien until now. His first thought was that it was too big for this crummy room. His second was that it probably knew a lot more about any given subject than Prescott did—including how to fight. He hoped the Hocq wouldn't make trouble. He didn't want to kill a being from another planet. It would look bad.

"Is he ready to move?"

"Ask him yourself," the kid said.

Prescott shoved him against the wall instead. It was hard enough that Jeremy's head made a good thump. "Don't get wise with me. I don't want anyone to get hurt, but if you or Frankenstein here pull any funny stuff, I'm not going to wait. Now, let me ask this again: Is he ready?"

The kid's eyes went wide with surprise when Prescott grabbed him, but narrowed quickly. The outlaw knew for a fact that he would hate to take him on in a fair fight . . . but this wasn't fair. He had guns on his side and he didn't let go.

"He seems to be all right," Jeremy said quietly. "I don't really know that much about him. He says he's not well . . . but he can move."

He let the boy go. "There, that wasn't hard, was it?"

"If you say so."

Canfield had come into the room. Prescott nodded at him to be patient. "Okay, kid, this is the program. I'm going to try to make a little deal for you two." He forced himself to look directly at the Hocq's masked face. "Can he understand me?" he said loudly.

"It is not necessary to shout," Harrek replied. "My sensors can detect the sounds of your heart beating."

Prescott didn't care at all for that remark. His heartbeat was his business, especially since at the moment it was pounding like an Indian drum. "Great. Okay, both of you listen: You, Jeremy, will take your friend here out front and put him in the comm jeep. Canfield'll show you. Once you're done with that, you get yourself into the wagon. We're going to be on the road in about ten minutes, and if you're good boys—both of you—you'll be home this afternoon." Prescott blinked. "Well, closer to home."

"Let's go, Harrek," Jeremy said. Prescott stood aside to let the creature pass. He had a hard time thinking of him as an intelligent being. To Prescott, Harrek looked more like a skinny bear in a white suit. A skinny bear with extra, snakelike arms where his knees should be.

When they were gone he left the bedroom himself and found Rickie stuffing his bedroll into his knapsack. "That thing going with us?"

"Yeah. Part of the way, anyway."

"Jesus, Rob—"

Prescott didn't let him finish the thought. He grabbed Rickie's long blond hair and held it painfully tight. "I wouldn't take any lip from the kid and I sure as hell won't take any from you. That *thing* and the kid are our tickets out of here. If you don't like the arrangements, you can start walking."

Rickie tried to smile. "Hey, no, Rob, everything's okay. Whatever you say."

"I know. You just keep forgetting." He released him, turned his back, and went outside.

Canfield was already wedged into the driver's seat of the comm jeep. It was a tighter fit than usual, with the alien in the back. The right front seat had been folded down to make room for the creature's legs. Prescott wondered if the creature would be able to grab the driver from behind. Or whether he would want to. "Canfield, come here a second."

"What is it?"

"I'll drive the comm jeep."

"Suit yourself."

"You drive lead."

Canfield got a quizzical expression on his face. "Okay . . . Mind if I ask why?"

"Because you're going to take the lead jeep and the wagon and go north. I'm going south with the alien."

Canfield was bright; you didn't have to draw him a picture. "Do we have to do it that way?"

"Yeah, I think so. I'll go south toward those choppers and get them on the radio. I'll tell them I've got the alien—what the hell, I'll put him on and let him tell them himself! They'll have to drop the quarantine at the bridge. Once you're across and free and clear, you let me know, and they'll get the alien back."

"What happens to you?"

"You know, that's a question that keeps popping into my head a lot."

"You're going to trust them, Rob? You know they've reneged on deals before."

"Yeah, but let's face it, this deal is sort of unique. You've got the alien here, for one thing—and from what we've heard on the radio, there's more than just CSA people involved on the other end." He sighed. "Besides, we don't have any options. This stuff has got to get home and Johnston's got to get to a doctor. I can't think of any other way to do both."

"Well, what about the kid?"

Prescott glanced at the loaded wagon. Rickie was driving with Stagger as shotgun. Jeremy rode in the back with Johnston and the others. The young prisoner watched Prescott warily, as if he knew he was the subject under discussion. "Do what you have to do," Prescott said quietly. "I don't have room to take him with me."

Then he slapped the hood of the jeep. "Okay, let's move it!"

CHAPTER 20

Outlaw Territory, Friday (Continued)

To Harrek, even considering his limited exposure to human beings, it was clear the outlaw Prescott was in a dangerous state of mind. In fact, he had come to resemble nothing so much as a First during a crisis—focused entirely on the problem at hand, devoting all energies, all memories, all skills to it. Harrek wished he could do the same himself.

As he waited in the jeep he took inventory. The worldline of his companion Lisa Marquez had ceased to be congruent to his own, and much earlier than all his careful projections. He regretted the failure of her brave mission on his behalf even more than he regretted the failure of his projections. He didn't even know if she had survived the crash. His sensors had been so overloaded during and immediately after the disaster that he had been unable to scan the wreckage for signs of life—or the lack thereof.

Then there was the young human Jeremy Clayton, whose worldline was now intertwined with Harrek's to an alarming extent. Harrek had begun to feel a certain amount of sympathy for the young Earth man, perhaps because Jeremy's social state and position had much in common with Harrek's: each was in the process of rejecting the society into which he had been born. They were between Castes.

He wanted to know if the human equivalent of ascent also resulted in death for those who attempted and failed. He suspected that it did.

Finally, Harrek was concerned about his own physical state, which had stabilized in the last pre-rashch stage. Another spell would bring on the terrible spasms of the fissioning process, which would leave Harrek debilitated for years. Now Harrek had accepted —indeed, had courted—this risk in refusing his injections, but only based upon projections that his terminal phase would occur after he was in safe hands . . . away from Boroz. The anxiety he had felt during the emergency flight had surely accelerated the process and nothing had occurred since to slow it. He could not enter rashch here. Aside from danger to himself, there was the health of the infant brother to consider. But Harrek was trapped for the moment, at the mercy of a rogue human.

The jeep, guided by the outlaw Prescott, moved slowly along the rutted road, reminding Harrek of a cautious beast of burden picking its way across a field. Strange how memories returned. Perhaps he was physically damaged in a way he could not detect. That thought disturbed him greatly. The sturdy pressure suit had protected him from serious injury in the crash. There was a property in the fabric which caused it to harden upon impact. It was a clever idea—one the Hocq did not possess—and yet another example of the wonders to be won if Boroz would release the Genesis material so that open exchange could occur.

Earth people might have something to teach the Hocq.

Harrek was not concentrating. Though the suit had protected him from the initial shock of the crash, and from the fire, the garment had suffered several tears, rendering it useless as a pressure suit. Since the accident, then, Harrek had been breathing the unfiltered air of Earth. This should not have been cause for worry: Hocq and human were similar enough biologically that each could survive in an atmosphere of comparable mixture and pressure. But the hazards of exposure to organic elements—allergens—all that was unknown.

At least his sensors operated with no apparent loss of efficiency. Harrek had guided Jeremy in a minor repair operation that ensured that. Thus he was able to monitor the conversations of the outlaw Prescott with his wounded companion, Johnston, with his rebellious underling, Rickie, with the loyal Canfield, and with Jeremy. Here was a fascinating Earth man—a true entrepreneur, perhaps, in audacity, a match for Boroz herself. Here was just the sort of Earth man for whom Harrek had searched . . . and now he was in no position to make use of him.

Harrek tried to get comfortable in the cramped back seat of the jeep, but shifting about only changed the loci of pain. The movement also alarmed the outlaw Prescott, who glanced over his shoulder and edged to one side of his seat.

"I am in pain," Harrek said.

Prescott kept his eyes on the road. "Sorry about that. We'll be stopping soon. You'll be able to get out then."

"Then you will make the transmission."

"That's right."

A transmission to Boroz, that was what Harrek foresaw. More than ever he needed to meditate, to float on the frail winds of a dream, to try to outguess Entropy. Whose worldlines were dominant? Where did they intersect? All Harrek could sense now was the overwhelming nearness of Boroz, and perhaps one or two others.

All else was darkness and pain.

"Did Lippert have any news on when the trucks would get here?" Shapiro asked.

He had just returned from escorting Boroz from the landing zone to the nearby farmyard, where he would be left to the mercy of the CSA press pool. Strauss had a hunch the reporters would find the Ambassador somewhat less transparent than the usual "highly placed source," which was why he had allowed the informal conference to proceed. He looked up from his comm unit, having spent the last half hour trying to reestablish contact with the civilized world and getting, for his troubles, nothing but CSA databases and some sitcom called "The Worker's Paradise," which obviously originated in Chicago. "Patience, Doug," he said. "Lippert told us it would be 'an hour to an hour and a half' when we were on the chopper. If you apply the Strauss Conversion Factor, which says that you always double an official time or cost estimate . . . let's just say that I don't expect to see any of those trucks for at least *another* hour."

Shapiro looked drawn and tired. He certainly had ample justification.

"Hey, why don't you just go down to that house, find a couch or something, and take a nap?"

Shapiro's eyes widened in a mixture of horror and desire. "Oh no, I couldn't. Really."

"Why not?" Strauss concentrated on powering down his lap unit while hiding a smile.

"Well . . . I wouldn't feel right just walking in on them. It's their *home.*"

Strauss closed the case with a loud snap. "Not at the moment it's not. Besides, according to Lippert these people have no official existence. They pay no taxes to the CSA, they provide no young people for the militia . . . do you think they're entitled to citizens' privileges?"

"I think I do, actually," Shapiro said, refusing to take the bait.

For the first time Strauss felt a genuine sense of respect toward his young assistant. He had guts, of course, but idealism, too—a rare combination. "To tell the truth, so do I," Strauss said. "In fact, I'm going to stroll on down there and see if I can't keep Lippert from arresting everybody in sight. Why don't you just sack out here in the chopper? It's a little cramped, but then, you're not likely to care."

"Thanks, I will."

Strauss took off across the lumpy field, passing close to the base of the ancient wind generator. Shapiro had first called attention to it but he was nowhere nearly old enough to appreciate the antiquity of the design . . . and the machine's importance to people like this. Why, they'd even built an access platform around the pod at the top. He wondered who among these dirty, sullen people had the brains to think of that, and do it.

These people, their generator, the helicopters . . . it all reminded him of the War.

He had been a military officer then, a first lieutenant in the Texas National Guard, just a month out of basic, a member of the team assigned to the massive refugee problem in the Rio Grande area after the Brownsville mess. That was the year when it seemed the whole world was against Texas . . . not only the Soviets and the Africans, but the Central States and California, too. All of them aimed their plague weapons and orbital beams at Texas. And one of them—to this day no one knew who—had used one on Brownsville.

Strauss had seen hundreds of half-starved brown-faced men,

women, and children, their lives and progeny threatened, all of them driven from their homes by a conflict in which they had not the slightest interest or investment. He had worked with them for months, interviewing, assigning, reprimanding, mediating, cajoling, commuting from one stinking camp to another in helicopters long in need of retrofitting. It was one thing to lose a comrade, a soldier, in a just war, because Strauss believed that some wars were just—but to see thousands of dead and dying civilians paying the price for super-power political games . . . it cost a man.

It took no great intuitive leap to see that a similar sick drama was being replayed on a smaller scale right here in the hills of Iowa. In less time than it took to set up TV cameras, Lippert had herded the dozen inhabitants into the living room of their big house, putting them under guard while he talked about his big find—an outlaw hideout!—pausing only for the occasional stand-up with the press.

It was worse than a shame, it was wrong. These people weren't outlaws. They were farmers, and poor ones at that. Their house showed no signs of being an outlaw dwelling. It was right out in the open. It had been standing for over a hundred years. It looked solid and lived in. The people themselves had no more weaponry than God gave Adam, and nothing resembling mechanized transport. Didn't Lippert remember that there were thousands of communes like this all over the Central States and Texas?

Strauss was beginning not to care whether they found Harrek or not. Let Boroz fume. Let the Hocq keep their damn Genesis File. We wouldn't know how to use it anyway . . .

"Colonel Lippert!"

Approaching the yard proper, Strauss saw a single CSA trooper marching two more hill people toward the house. The yard was too crowded with lounging soldiers and press for the new prisoners to pass safely, so Lippert and his aide had to come out to meet them.

"I found these two sneaking out of the barn," the trooper said.

Strauss saw before him a weathered, wild-eyed woman, and a stooped old man with dried mud on his clothes. He was about to write them off as typical refugees when he caught sight of the old man's eyes glinting behind ancient glasses. His face contained pure defiance and animal cunning.

"Good job, Sergeant," Lippert was saying. Teri Pedroza and her cameraman were right behind him. "It seems," the militia commander announced to his imaginary global audience, "that we've captured two more members of this outlaw community—"

"We aren't outlaws," the old man snapped. "And take that thing out of my back." He was referring to the guard's autorifle.

Lippert smiled condescendingly. "You're only the tenth person to tell me that."

"Then it's high time you started paying attention," the man said. "We've been living peacefully up here for over sixty years. This is *our* land. *You're* the outlaws—"

"That'll be enough," Lippert said. "Take them into the house. Gently, of course." The gracious host turned and smiled and, as he did, the old man stumbled and fell . . . right in front of the camera. *The old fraud!* Strauss thought. Then he corrected himself: the old man was hurt.

The woman began to moan. Lippert had the presence of mind—or theater, since the cameras were now on him—to call for a medic.

While the old man was being carried across the yard, Strauss happened to glance toward the barn, about a hundred yards away. Someone—a human with a pronounced limp—was hobbling down the hill and not being leisurely about it. He wished he had a pair of binoculars; there was something familiar about that walk, even if you allowed for the limp . . .

"Captain Strauss!"

A soldier was calling him. Lippert had disappeared into the house. He must have been in a hurry.

"What is it?"

"There's a message coming in over the radio—"

Strauss ran for the house and caught up with Lippert. Both of them stared at the combat comm unit.

"—name is Rob Prescott. To repeat, I have the Hocq named Harrek with me. He's alive and well, but I'll destroy him unless my instructions are followed to the letter—"

Lippert looked sick. "Everybody shut up," Strauss said. "I've got to hear this."

Then he realized what the noise was. Outside, half a dozen heavily armed CSA personnel carriers were rolling into the yard.

"What the hell do we do now?" Rickie said, kicking gravel as he paced along the road.

"Shut up," was all Canfield told him. The older outlaw was busy peering through his scope toward Slougham Bridge and the Turkey River, which now lay safely behind them.

Rickie made a face for Stagger's benefit, and for Jeremy, who, from his position perched atop a stack of boxes in the back of the wagon, had the best view of the bunch. Halfway up a gentle, wooded hill and pulled off to the shoulder of a well-paved road, they faced south toward the river, toward the hills that surrounded Arrowsmith. They had covered a stretch of open ground at a rate Jeremy thought quite comparable to Lisa's Hurricane. The sun, which had been dipping in and out of the clouds all morning, had finally given up and gone under. In the reduced light the little Turkey looked cold and mean. Nevertheless, it was hard for Jeremy to be fully taken with the view: he was too aware that next to him in the wagon the outlaw Johnston was dying.

Rickie came over to the wagon and leaned next to Stagger. "What do you suppose is taking Rob so long?"

"Maybe he stopped to take a leak."

Rickie laughed, but was still worried. Even Jeremy knew that Prescott's broadcast was late. By the time the convoy had reached Slougham Bridge he knew most of the details of the escape plan. It was all Stagger and Rickie talked about.

They were to have drawn up to the bridge, waiting safely behind the turn until Prescott made contact with the CSA strike force and got the roadblock lifted. Once that was accomplished, they were to cross the river as quickly as possible and get into the hills on the north side, where Canfield could radio the leader that they were in the clear. Only then would Prescott release the Hocq. "He'll probably just point him in the right direction and tell him to start walking," Rickie had said. "Give himself a head start, if he can."

"He'll need it," Stagger had said. "Rob's sneaky, but you've got to be more than sneaky to get out of something like this—"

It had seemed to Jeremy that they were about to discuss his situation when Canfield returned running from the river. "There's nobody *there!*" So they'd raced across the bridge, passing the cold hulk of the bombed-out carrier.

"Maybe we should call Rob," Stagger said. He and Rickie were jittery, pointing their weapons all over the place, including at each other.

Canfield gave up on the scope and came back toward them. "Because he said he'd call *us."* He sounded tired. "He probably won't be listening, anyway. He's got his hands full driving the jeep and keeping an eye on Frankenstein." He climbed into the wagon. "How's Johnston doing?"

"He's out cold," Jeremy said.

"Yeah, we gave him a lot of stuff to help him sleep." Canfield touched the sick man's forehead. "Jesus." He yanked aside the blanket and felt for the artery in Johnston's neck. Then, with a look of resignation, he put his ear to the man's chest.

He sat back. "Well, at least it's over for him." He blinked. "I recruited him."

"I'm sorry," Jeremy said.

"Isn't your fault," Canfield told him. "Stagger! Rickie! Get your butts up here!"

But Stagger, who had been poking around in Canfield's jeep, was waving. "Here he is! I've got him!"

Canfield jumped down and ran for the comm unit. Jeremy followed; he wasn't anxious to share a wagon with a dead outlaw.

"—Don't anyone try to find me," Prescott was saying. "Don't even think about it. If I get feeling paranoid, the Hocq gets killed."

"He already sounds paranoid," Rickie said.

Prescott was breathing hard, like a man who had just run up a hill.

"I want safe passage for my men, which means that I want all roadblocks lifted from Guthrie Road, Slougham Bridge, and Highway 56. When I get word from my people that they're clear, the Hocq will be released, not before."

Another voice came on the frequency, but it was too broken and faint to be heard by Jeremy and the outlaws. Prescott heard them, though, because he kept up his end of the conversation. He even put

Harrek on the line long enough for the alien's unmistakable rasp to
be identified. Then Prescott said, "And just to move things along a
little, let's put a time limit of ninety minutes on lifting those patrols.
If I don't hear that they're gone by then . . . well, I'm just going to
have to make alternate arrangements—and they won't include the
Hocq. I'll call again when I hear from my people. Out." The transmission ended.

"Now he's going to change his location so they can't triangulate.
He'll find another crest," Canfield said. "Give him fifteen or twenty
minutes and then we'll call him, let him know the good news about
the bridge."

"What's to stop them from triangulating *us?*" Rickie asked.

"Because we call Rob on a different, prearranged freak, that's
what," Canfield said nastily. "For a guy who's got all the answers,
Rickie, you sure don't know very much."

Rickie's face sprouted a pair of red patches. Jeremy thought there
would be a fight, but Canfield changed the subject, grabbing a shovel
from the jeep. "Come on, let's do what we can for Johnston while we
have a few minutes." Rickie went with him, shooting a dirty look
toward Jeremy as he did.

Stagger stayed at the jeep. Was that a smile on his face? Jeremy
couldn't tell and didn't, in fact, want to know. The little outlaw
climbed out of the driver's seat.

He left the key in the ignition.

Jeremy thought his heart would explode. He was paralyzed, confused: Should he run? Was Stagger going to kill him now, while *he*
had a few minutes?

Fifteen minutes until Canfield called Prescott.

Stagger had a duffel bag out on the ground and was searching in it,
whistling to himself as if Jeremy did not exist. He bent over, turning
his back.

Jeremy slammed him into the side of the jeep, then got a good grip
on Stagger's shoulders and banged the outlaw's head hard against
the panel a second time, leaving a dent in the metal and making a
dull thud. Stagger must have been completely surprised: he didn't
react at all, except to give a mild cry when his head hit the jeep.

Jeremy scrambled into the seat and twisted the key the way he'd seen Canfield do it all morning. The engine START light flashed on. What next? *What next?* That stick next to the steering wheel—move it. Push on that pedal by your right foot. It had to work—

"*Hey!*"

Canfield and Rickie. Jeremy stepped hard on the wrong pedal, then frantically pressed the other with the correct foot, turning the wheel at the same time.

The jeep lurched and spun onto the road, spraying gravel behind it. Jeremy was glad that the road ahead looked straight, because he had nothing resembling confidence in his ability to control the machine as it raced forward. But in a few moments he was sure of the difference between the brake and the accelerator, and the steering wasn't that tough to understand . . . and he was *free*, barreling down the road, away from the outlaws, out of sight. The shouting faded.

Now he had a moment to consider what he'd done. His chest started to heave. He didn't think he'd killed Stagger—he was sure he hadn't run over him. Then he remembered what had happened to Neil and didn't feel that sorry anymore.

He kept to the same road for what seemed like a long time but couldn't have been more than a few minutes. Ten minutes, tops. He wondered how his escape would screw up Prescott's plans for Harrek—and for the outlaws, since he'd taken their radio. For that matter, how had he changed his own plans? Where could he go now? The way back to Arrowsmith was closed to him, and he was not about to start searching for a CSA patrol. Or should he? Would they be able to do something in the time that remained to Harrek?

The road grew more level as he drove along the crest of a ridge. The vegetation here was so dense it forced him to slow down periodically to maneuver around fallen branches. But each obstacle negotiated gave him more familiarity with the jeep. It was just a machine, after all, and he understood machines. He was beginning to think he could understand anything, given time.

Up ahead the road split in two.

Jeremy slowed down enough so that he could take the left fork safely. If he had his directions right, the left fork would take him

west. Sure enough, within a minute the jeep started to descend from
the hills, breaking completely out of the trees.

He almost drove off the road.

Spread before him was a flat, cultivated field that looked, even
from his altitude, as if it might stretch to the end of the world. And
in the distance stood a series of buildings more massive than anything he'd dreamed. But it wasn't the buildings or the impossibly
large field that stunned him . . . it was the row of giant wind generators that bordered that field. The machines grew larger and larger
the closer he got, until he literally drove right under one whose huge
legs straddled the road. High above him the big-bladed prop turned
lazily.

Tears came to his eyes. It must be the wind . . .

He wanted to stop, but there was no time. He had to do something
for Harrek, and maybe Ben and Elizabeth and Heather, too. He had
to get *home*.

Shortly he passed the fenced and guarded entrance to the complex
of buildings. MARTIN FARMS the sign said.

Not much farther down the road he saw another sign:

> KELLEHER'S MERCHANDISE MART
> 5 MILES AHEAD
> Junction I-56 and 3rd Street
> IN WEST UNION!

CHAPTER 21

Arrowsmith, Friday Afternoon

"Who's the spokesman here?"

Ben raised his head at the sound of the soldier's voice. The movement made him ill, probably because, along with the others, he had been sitting on the floor of the common room since the arrival of the CSA force two hours ago.

"Ben, wake up." Elizabeth was talking to him. She sat next to him on the floor.

The soldier heard her. "Ben Clayton?"

Now he had to stand up. "That's me," he said. Fortunately the dizziness passed quickly. Outside in the yard soldiers could be seen, the same people who had herded them in here like cattle. Ben hadn't cared for that, especially when they'd carried Dan past the door and wouldn't let anyone help. Ben sized up the guard: he was a head taller and a lot heavier, but in spite of the way he felt, he considered taking him on.

"Are you willing to speak for these people?" the soldier repeated.

Ben shrugged. "I just live here." Everyone who lived at Hill House was in the room, with the exception of Jeremy. Ben was content to let any one of them be the "spokesman," whatever that was.

But the others urged him on. "Go ahead, Ben." "Get us out of here." Even Elizabeth was nodding to him.

"I guess I'm your man," he told the soldier. The others moved aside for him as best they could. The soldier, too, stepped out of his way.

The foyer was crowded with even more people than the common room, which didn't seem possible. Some were bluejackets, but others carried equipment that kept finding its way in front of Ben's nose as he pushed through the bodies. Questions were shouted at him: "Are you an outlaw?" "Have you been sheltering the Hocq?" "Have you been harmed?"

He didn't know what they were talking about, so he said nothing, letting his guard steer him farther into the house to the kitchen.

"In there, please," the soldier said, taking up a position blocking the entrance.

It was less crowded in the kitchen, but still uncomfortable. The creature that Jeremy had run off with was standing by the back door, damn near as big as a horse and with arms like the branches of an oak. There were others in the kitchen, too: a pair of older soldiers and a stocky man with a ridiculous bag over one shoulder.

"My name is Tim Strauss," the thick man said, holding out his hand. "I apologize for the misunderstandings and inconvenience."

Ben shook, not taking his eyes off the other creature. "Ben Clayton." He was introduced to a Colonel Lippert and to a second soldier, identified only as "the colonel's aide."

"And this," Strauss said, getting to the creature at last, "is Ambassador Boroz of the Hocq." The creature made no response. Its lower arms were waving up and down, but they had been doing that since Ben walked in. "Please have a seat, Ben. Do you have a title, something the others call you?"

He sat down, surprised at how good it felt. "We don't go in for titles here."

"I thought not," Strauss said, smiling. "Well, Colonel, do you have anything to add—or should I continue with the briefing?"

To Ben, Colonel Lippert looked like a very unhappy man. He sucked air into his face, then let it out, a lot of effort to produce a mild, "No, sir."

"Thank you, Colonel." Strauss removed his shoulder bag and set it on the table. "Okay, Ben, here's our problem. We need help from someone who knows this land well enough to walk it in his sleep. As the . . . leader of this community, you're the obvious choice. But first, I suppose, you want to know why you should even bother."

"That's right. I'd like to hear a little about that." He coughed once, hard, the first one in hours. "I'd also like to know what this fellow"— he pointed at Boroz —"did with my son."

"What about your son, Ben?" Strauss said.

Answering Strauss's questions, Ben told him what had happened in the past few days. "Ben, Boroz did nothing with your son or with any other member of your community. She only arrived here this morning. The person you saw was Boroz's younger brother . . . the person all of us are looking for. That's why we need your help."

Ben found himself eager to help Strauss, partly because of his relaxed, confident manner, and partly because he seemed anxious to solve the problem. "Come to think of it, you're right," he said. "This one is taller and heavier than the one that rode off with Jeremy."

Boroz leaned toward Ben. "Do you know Harrek's present location? Can you find him for us?"

"This man has said he'll help us, Excellency—" Strauss started to say.

"I've waited enough!" Boroz announced. "I'm returning to the helicopter! If Harrek is not found immediately, I will contact my ship and we will find him." The alien burst out of the kitchen into a waiting knot of reporters. Ben realized that the alien's presence had made him nervous.

"Captain Strauss?" It was the colonel's aide this time, sounding more unhappy than his boss.

"This won't take much longer. Ben, we've been searching for Boroz's brother since Monday night. An hour ago we received a message from an outlaw named Prescott who claims to be holed up somewhere not far from here with that alien. He wants us to remove the roadblocks we've set up around this area so that his men can escape." Strauss smiled without humor. "It seems we captured them by mistake."

Lippert grunted. "But," Strauss continued, "we've already dropped those roadblocks, and I'm afraid it must have thrown a monkey wrench into their plans, because we haven't heard from Prescott since. Now, we have a rough idea where he was when he sent his message, and he couldn't have moved far in that time. But he threatened to kill Boroz's brother . . . and, as you can imagine, that is a problem for us."

It didn't make much sense to Ben. "Why in hell should the big one be acting like that? Aren't you helping him out?"

"Her," the aide said.

"Well, we are, and a human being would realize that, but Boroz comes from a race that has very little in common with ours. They look on us the way we'd look on cattle, or smart dogs. We don't really know what brought them to Earth and we don't know what they're capable of doing if they get angry. But to be perfectly honest with you, they have the ability to blow up the whole planet. We don't really know what kind of superweapons they might have—"

"—Except that they're a damn sight better than ours!" the aide remarked.

"It's safe to assume they are, yes. I'd had to find out the hard way. And there's an additional factor here: I said the missing alien was Boroz's brother. That isn't strictly the case. They're related, all right, but they're what we call conjugants: they reproduce by fission once in their lives, literally splitting themselves in two. It's a relationship so close we can't imagine it. But think how you feel about your missing son, and triple it. So you see, we're being forced to move before we're really ready. If I showed you a position on a map of the area, could you lead my men there without being detected? It's our only hope of ending this stupid situation, and of rescuing your son, too."

"Well," Ben said, "that depends on where this outlaw's got to. It isn't hard to sneak up on someone in this country. There's lots of cover. But before I take a look at *anything*, I will have to have something from you people."

"What's that?" Lippert was suspicious.

Ben was taking nothing more from these guys. "I want you to get these soldiers and these machines out of here, out of this house, right now. I want you to let everyone come and go as they please and leave 'em the hell alone. Until that happens, I'm going to sit right here where it's warm."

"Now just a damn minute—" The colonel was getting loud.

"Amnesty granted," Strauss said quickly. "Colonel, get your troops off this man's land now. Move the helicopters, and especially get those reporters out of here."

"Captain, I think we ought to—"

"We ought to do this as quickly as possible," Strauss said coldly. "Time's awasting. Ben, would it be all right if we moved them across the highway until we're done?"

"I suppose that'll have to do for now. But by sundown I want them all the way out of here."

"You have my word they will be." To Lippert, Strauss said, "Go, Colonel. And get an assault squad up here while you're at it." The soldiers hesitated for a moment, then went outside shouting orders.

Strauss pointed to the screen he had set up on the table. It gave a view of the whole community as if someone had lifted you high in the sky and let you look down. There, to the north, was the twisting Turkey River and a road cutting across it. South of that, hills, woods, another road, and Hill House.

"Is that us there?" Ben asked.

"Sure is," Strauss said. "It's based on digital satellite imaging a few hours old, of course, but the computer extrapolates from more recent inputs, allowing for changing sun angles, time of day, things like that. I told it to allow for a heavy cloud cover today which, as you can see, takes away the shadows and makes it very difficult for strange eyes to judge heights."

A circle appeared on the screen at a spot northwest of Hill House, about halfway between it and the outskirts of West Union, which was itself visible in the upper left-hand corner. "That's the approximate position of the outlaw when he made his broadcast . . . an hour and ten minutes ago. There was some slight dopplering in the signal, so we know he was moving. The circle indicates the farthest he could have gotten since, assuming nominal jeep performance."

Ben continued to study the wonderful map, more for his own amusement than out of any real need. He had an idea, though. "Can you take that circle off the map?"

It disappeared. "Now put it back on."

He thought for a moment, trying to move his mind's eye down from the clouds to the ground . . . He'd be on Arrowsmith Road, for sure. Where would he hide if he wanted to be close to Hill House, but still be able to see anyone searching for him?

He put his finger on the screen, which felt surprisingly fragile. "Right here," he said. "It looks like he'd be on Willow Ridge."

The colonel's aide had returned. "Captain Strauss, we've got the assault team waiting at the road. The rest of the units will be deployed along the highway. The helicopters are going into the air, and they'll stand off to the north until needed. We've alerted the units on the quarantine. He can't get away."

"But he can still kill Harrek. Where's Boroz?"

"In chopper two, with your aide."

"Well, let's do it," Strauss said, closing the map screen and stuffing it in his bag. "Ben?"

Elizabeth had come to the kitchen door. "Dan's sick," she said.

"Is that the elderly man who fell?" Strauss asked. "Don't worry, we're looking after him, if that's all right."

"They'll help," he told Elizabeth. "I'm going with these people for a while."

This time her worry was for him. "Be careful," she said. Ben wished he had a moment to talk to her, but there would be time for that. They would make time.

The next thing he knew he was out in the yard and Strauss was hurrying up across the field toward the helicopters.

"Can you slow down a little?"

Jeremy had to shout, as the jeep's wheels hit the ground with a terrifying shock after going airborne over the last bump.

"You said you were in a hurry!" Red Hoerner shouted back. "Don't worry, this little s.o.b. can take it!"

They were tearing up Slougham Road with the Turkey on their left and the bluffs on their right. Jeremy had never noticed how shallow and rocky the little river was, or how rough an apparently smooth road could become if you drove over it fast enough. He was grateful when Hoerner eased off the accelerator. The noise diminished so they could talk without screaming. "I hope you don't get in trouble," Jeremy said.

"The job? Hell with it. Kenny can handle things for a while. They owe me a lot of vacation there, anyway. If Janet doesn't like it, she can get somebody else." He was grinning. "I'd quit a couple of jobs for the chance to drive a baby like this."

Jeremy was glad Hoerner was happy about it. He wasn't so sure himself. "Well, thanks for helping me out."

"Hey, I couldn't let you come up here and fight it out with a bunch of bluejackets all by yourself—especially if they're assholes from downstate. You need someone to ride shotgun, kid."

"Is that it?" Hoerner had "borrowed" a pair of blazer rifles and a pistol from Kelleher's without so much as asking where Jeremy was going or what he planned to do.

"Looks that way," Hoerner said. "The militia punks were all over town last night, raising hell, and from what I hear, they're all over the hills today. You didn't pick up this jeep in the lottery—you want to tell me what's going on?"

"Do you remember that woman in the Hurricane? And the creature inside? They're up here." Jeremy took a deep breath, having come to an important decision. "We're going to help them."

"Suits me fine, kid. Point the way."

The key was finding Prescott before he could hurt Harrek, or before Harrek got any sicker. But finding Prescott—Jeremy wished he knew more about the comm unit in the jeep, sure that it held a clue to the outlaw's whereabouts. He might even be able to contact him directly. But this was no time for a beginner's course in communications . . . He would just have to think like Prescott. Canfield had said he was going to reach a "hilltop."

There was only one ridge prominent enough to be called a hilltop anywhere near Sun House. "Keep going till we get to the bridge," Jeremy told Hoerner. "Then head for the highest ground you see. We're going to have to climb Willow Ridge."

CHAPTER 22

Outlaw Territory, Friday Afternoon

Rob Prescott leveled his blazer at Harrek's back and took a long drag from his second joint. Ordinarily he abstained from dope on the road . . . but this was turning out to be a special day.

They'd be coming up Arrowsmith Road any minute now—half the Third Division, if they followed normal CSA tactics. It was his own damn fault, too, for not making some sort of second broadcast, but the lack of any response from Canfield about the river crossing had shaken him. It was clear that the bluejackets had gotten the convoy, and that either they didn't think he would snuff the alien, or they didn't care.

A more sinister possibility was that they didn't think Prescott *could* kill the Hocq. Suppose Frankenstein was really impervious to Earth weapons?

He had half a mind to test the theory.

Enough paranoia. He ground the roach in the ashtray. He hadn't survived all these years in his profession to end up like this . . . half stoned, crying about his bad luck. Think, man.

"What do you say, Frank?" he asked Harrek, who stood several feet away, directly in front of the jeep.

"I have not been speaking," the alien replied.

Prescott thought that was a pretty funny remark, under the circumstances. "Well, then, what *have* you been doing? What do you people do for fun, anyway?"

"I've been meditating."

"Like it?"

"At one time I found it very worthwhile. I would not say that such is presently the case."

Prescott got out of the jeep and moved toward the crest of Willow Ridge. He kept glancing back at Harrek. Even though they were hidden here beneath a trio of old pines that had long ago poked out of the rocky ridgetop, they had an unobstructed view at least a mile north and south, all along the winding hollow road. There was also a clear field of fire down the eastern slope. The hilltop, in fact, would have been an impregnable defensive position . . . if you had a dozen armed men and something less than six hundred militia and several attack helicopters against you. The site's only flaw was the heavy brush cover on the western slope, and the easy access from that direction. Prescott had been able to drive up that slope without much trouble.

Well, the ninety minutes was up. It was getting on toward late afternoon. If the CSA held off long enough, it might be dark enough for Prescott to ditch the jeep and the alien and make a run for it on foot. He wished now that he'd made that second call to the CSA commander, but he'd been too afraid of blowing what small mystery remained regarding his location. They had all this weird tracking equipment.

What in God's name had happened to Canfield, anyway? Open to their prearranged frequency, the radio hissed . . . and gave nothing. Maybe he should call them again.

He walked back to the jeep.

Harrek turned slightly. "Someone is coming."

In the space of a second Prescott weighed two options and chose the smarter one. "Which way?"

"The direction of the sun."

"Okay, keep quiet and don't move." He shut off the radio and ducked behind the jeep.

Flattening out, he crawled uphill to the base of the tree immediately to the west, then looked through the fragrant branches that reached all the way to the ground. He could see nothing but trees, which were scattered here and there across the bowl-shaped crest. But someone was out there . . . the alien had said so.

He would just have to wait and pray that the CSA strike force didn't drive up his ass while he had his back turned.

Movement! He fired a bolt from the blazer, singeing needles and bark off a pine halfway across the hilltop. Over there! He rolled and fired again, this time kicking up a spray of dirt.

Where were they?

Frantically, he slithered back to the jeep.

"Don't move," a voice told him. He didn't.

"Drop the gun."

He dropped the gun, sliding it away.

"This way."

Prescott rolled to his right. There was Harrek, and beside him, looking mean, with a rifle pointed his way, was that damn farm kid, Jeremy Clayton.

Before Prescott could say a word another figure appeared from behind him, a heavy-set, redheaded guy wearing a jacket that said GARNAVILLO CUBS. "Is he the only one?" the redhead asked, out of breath.

"Yeah," Jeremy said, "but we're going to have some other people to worry about if we don't get off this hill. Harrek, are you okay?"

"For the moment, I am functioning."

"I hope that's a 'yes.' Get in the jeep, please." The kid waved the rifle at Prescott. "Come here. You're going to do some more driving."

"Whatever you say." He got in the driver's seat. He could not stop looking toward that western approach, expecting at any moment to see a horde of bluejackets swarming up at him.

"We have to get Harrek out of here," Jeremy said.

"Why? Your soldier buddies'll be along any minute."

The kid gave him a strange look. "I don't have any soldier buddies."

"Oh? Then what happened to my men?—"

"Hey!" That was the redhead shouting. He ran toward the jeep, tripped on a rock but kept going. "They're coming, man, a whole mess of them!" He threw himself into the jeep on top of Harrek.

"Soldiers?" the kid said.

"Yeah. With armor."

The kid ordered, "Prescott, take us down the hill."

It was crazy, but he gunned the engine and took the vehicle over the lip. "Everybody hold on!" The redhead was tossing equipment out the back and trying to wrap himself around the rollbar. The Hocq took up most of the room.

The first good bump almost turned them over. Then they hit an easy stretch for about twenty yards, zipping through some hillside meadow. They might be able to make it, if they could only reach Arrowsmith Road—

"Keep going!" Jeremy yelled.

Then tiny lightning bolts began to strike all around them. Prescott felt the wheel slip as the jeep dug into a rut, just when he needed to maneuver. They went up on two wheels and were no sooner back on all four when the jeep pitched nose first into a ditch.

The impact bruised them all, but not severely. Prescott managed to grab his spare pistol and get out of the jeep before anyone could stop him. *A real outlaw would shoot these guys,* he thought. He let himself roll down the hillside, round and round, like a child. Up the hill a handful of blue soldiers was silhouetted against the afternoon sky. They were all after him, it seemed.

He got up. It wasn't that far to the road! And cover—a place to hide!

Suddenly a chopper roared overhead, close enough for the wash to knock the breath out of him. He stumbled and fell, rolled again, but managed to point the pistol at the fat targets up the hill. He squeezed off a pair of bolts—

Another chopper zoomed up the hollow. He ducked.

Now! Prescott jumped to his feet and ran for his life, aiming for the base of the hill, which ended in a ledge that hung over the road. His arms and legs hurt so much he wanted to throw up. There was a burn in the middle of his back, where a blazer bolt had nicked him. Nothing to it; he could run all day, if they'd let him.

As he hit the ledge something punched him right in that same sore place. He went flying out over the road and the falling took forever.

CHAPTER 23

Arrowsmith, Friday Evening

"I think they're leaving," the woman at the window said, crossing her arms as she turned. Her name was Heather, she had said. Heather was probably all of seventeen, freckled, her long red hair done in a single braid . . . and pregnant, though it was hard to tell under the baggy jeans and coat. "It's about time."

Lisa Marquez watched the helicopters whirl into the evening sky with relief and fear. She was very happy that she was safe from the soldiers for the moment, but, really, how much safer was she with these people? Hadn't they nearly killed her last night?

She had to admit that today, so far, they had been nothing but kind. First Brandy, then the old man. It was if last night did not exist. Maybe it didn't. Maybe she had dreamed it all. Considering her accomplishments in the field of espionage, it was probably best for her to depend on the kindness of strangers.

"Will you be all right for a moment while I go downstairs?" Heather asked. "There are some more people coming down from the hill."

"I'll be fine," Lisa said, though it hurt just to talk.

"Don't try to get out of bed. I'm going to see if I can get Elizabeth to take a look at you."

Lisa had no desire to disobey, though she wasn't sure how anxious she was to have Elizabeth—whoever that was—"look" at her. Her left leg and ankle still hurt like the devil, primarily from that ridiculous run down the hill which, to Lisa's surprise, had actually worked. She had one or two cracked ribs and, worst of all, had inhaled smoke and fumes in the fire.

Nevertheless, she was lucky to be alive. She was lucky she hadn't gotten the fans up to full speed before the rocket hit them, lucky it had been snowing enough to damp the fire quickly, lucky Brandy Kramer had found her wrapped in Harrek's torn tent near the wreckage early that morning, dreaming she was back in Brownsville, hiding with Mom. Only this time, when the sirens blared, a four-armed alien was with them.

At least her sickroom was pleasant. It had natural light, which she liked. The walls, floor, and ceiling were all natural hardwood that looked tough enough to stand up to a Gulf hurricane, yet warm enough to keep out the midwestern winter.

My God, would she be here all winter? Would she be here the rest of her life? What about the Genesis File?

She forced herself to sit up, gaining a view out the window. The house on the hill wasn't that far away, in spite of Lisa's earlier certainty that she had walked almost a mile from there to here. Obviously she'd been confused. Thank God she had been able to understand when the old man told her, "We're going to set up a little distraction here, while you skedaddle down the hill. Ask for a girl named Heather and tell her Dan sent you. Then tell her to keep everybody at home until they hear from me or Ben Clayton. Can you remember that?"

She'd have tried to memorize the Austin phone book if it would get her away from CSA troops. And it had worked.

But what had happened to Harrek, and to Jeremy? Her memory of the time between the crash and Brandy's arrival was fuzzy. All she knew was that they were gone when she awoke . . .

Some people who were obviously not from around here were coming down the hill toward the lower house. Lisa got more and more nervous until she realized that they were not soldiers. That must be why Heather had left, to see the strangers. It was always like that in—

There was a news team . . . a man with a portapack camera following a tiny, dark-skinned woman. Lisa put her hand to her mouth and found that she wanted to giggle hysterically. *Teri?* Teri was supposed to be in *Denver!*

She began to pound on the window. "Teri!" she screamed. "Teri, up here! It's me, Lisa!"

"Are you well enough to talk?"

Harrek turned slightly so that one of his lesser arms could reach the talk switch on the speaker. "Yes."

"Thank you. Someone will be in to see you." The voice belonged to Harrek's human nurse, a man of middle age who had remained at the monitoring station outside Harrek's chamber throughout the early evening. Harrek was grateful for the dedication. The chamber itself, he had been told on arrival, was normally used for the delivery of human infants. A row of crèches had been pushed aside to make room for this strange visitor. The idea that a number of human newborn could be kept here at the same time was amusing and startling to Harrek. Newborn Hocq conjugants had to be separated from each other at rashch, since the trauma often caused the now-weakened and eviscerated one to try to kill the newborn. Harrek had always suspected that the cause of the lifelong animosity between Boroz and him resulted from their being separated too late . . .

No matter. It was his turn now, free at last of that torn and foul protective suit, no longer obliged to suffer torture inside cramped vehicles designed only for humans. He had been able to exercise properly for the first time in days and soon, perhaps, he would sleep. Only then would he be capable of fully judging his situation . . . only then would he be ready for his rashch.

There was a visitor outside, another human male, who convinced the nurse to let him enter. Harrek recognized the visitor as Shapiro, one of the humans accompanying the original mission.

Shapiro inquired after Harrek's health in ritual Hocq fashion and received the ritual positive—and untrue—reply. Then he said, in his own language, "I thought it would be a good idea if we talked before circumstances prevent it. I . . . ah . . . I've been sent to help you, if I can. If there's anything you require, just tell me."

"Thank you for your concern," Harrek said. "I'm quite sure that my sister is attending to my future comfort even as we speak."

"That was one of the things I wanted to discuss. Boroz will be here shortly and, frankly, we'll have a tough time keeping her out."

"Don't try. Her beautiful anger shines its brightest when it has a single victim."

The nervous young man sat down, the ghost of a smile on his lips. "Very well, then, to other matters. I've been sent to inform you, Secretary, that you are currently under arrest by the Central States of America on a charge of illegal entry. As an accessory, actually. Of course, as a diplomat you have immunity, but CSA law permits them to hold you for forty-eight hours for questioning."

"Is this necessary? My testimony, as an accessory, is useless unless someone is formally charged. Do these strange people prosecute the dead?"

"If you're referring to Lisa Marquez, Secretary, she's alive. She surrendered to CSA troops a little while ago. That was another subject we were to discuss. She's injured—in fact, she's in a room on the second floor of this hospital right now—but very much alive, and *very* subject to prosecution. My government is attempting to have her extradited to the People's Republic."

"But you are Texan." His companion had survived!

"Texas has no extradition treaty with the Central States. The People's Republic does." He cleared his throat. "I'm sorry. I don't want to tire you with trivia."

Harrek had not found the discussion to be trivial. Discussions of status were always in order. At the moment, "temporary prisoner of the Central States" was all he could lay claim to.

The nurse reappeared. "Mr. Shapiro? That program you wanted to watch is on. Channel Six."

"Thank you. Excuse me, Secretary." Shapiro went to a TV in the corner and turned it on. The sound carried clearly to Harrek's pallet and, after a request, Shapiro turned the set so that Harrek could see it, too.

"*. . . National Guard units captured a missing extraterrestrial today near Waterloo following a wild cross-country chase and a firefight which left one man dead and several people injured. We have a report from CBS News . . .*"

On the screen the camera—shooting from a helicopter flying fast and low—swooped over Willow Ridge and a group of soldiers and dropped down the hill toward a fleeing jeep, which careened across the field of view for only a moment. A second shot, from a more stable position, showed the jeep wedged nose first into a crevice. A team of soldiers rushed toward it, away from the camera.

A new voice said: "*. . . The outlaw was killed while two others captured with the Hocq were unhurt. A National Guard personnel carrier suffered a direct hit, slightly wounding three troopers . . .*"

Harrek watched impassively. The third shot, this one from a handheld camera, showed Harrek being helped out of the jeep by Jeremy. The camera lingered on them.

He hadn't known just how bad he looked.

"*. . . Still unexplained are the alien's reasons for his escape, or for the surrender of the fugitive Texan official a few hours later. Teri Pedroza, CBS News.*"

Shapiro shut off the set. "That's enough for now. As you can see, there's been quite a lot of interest in you and Lisa, in your story. Right now a couple of news teams are camped by the front door waiting to jump anyone who comes out."

The nurse returned again, this time looking a bit frantic, and spoke urgently to Shapiro.

"There's nothing I can do about it," Shapiro said. "We can hardly barricade the door."

Harrek stopped listening to them, concerned more with an uncontrollable quickening in his respiration rate. The constant dull ache spreading from his head to his swollen joints suddenly blossomed into full-scale agony. He arched off the pallet on four arms and cried out once, then again.

Just as suddenly it passed, though it left a residual pain that Harrek knew would burn again and again, at decreasing intervals, until his body split in two . . . His rashch had begun.

"I'll get the doctor," the nurse said.

"Don't bother," Shapiro told him. "There isn't a doctor on this planet who could help. Get Tim Strauss—"

Then the door burst open and Boroz entered, wearing her protective suit. The two humans backed out of her way as she advanced on Harrek, who was too wracked with pain and nausea to care.

Boroz hovered over him, huge and powerful. After a moment she summoned Shapiro. "We require privacy."

"Can we help?"

"No. Leave."

When they were gone, Harrek found the strength to speak. *"Welcome, sister."* He used the People's language.

"You have been treacherous," Boroz said. *"You have betrayed the mission. You have misused the Knowledge."*

"Untrue." Harrek could feel another spasm building. *"I have solved our problem. I have found a worthy recipient."*

"Interesting," Boroz said, stripping off her suit. *"A matter for further discussion, at a more appropriate time. Lie still. I will assist you."*

CHAPTER 24

West Union, CSA, Friday Morning

Only when the first light of the pale star of Earth brightened the window of the hospital room did Boroz admit the two humans who had kept vigil all night. One was a doctor, the other the human Strauss. Both men wore surgical masks which hid their no doubt startled expressions. Boroz was sorry she couldn't see them.

What the men saw was one adult Hocq hovering over a giant-sized bed upon which rested two smaller, fuzzier, unformed versions. "It is over," Boroz told them. "The newborn will be quiet for some time yet. I will need food, equipment and supplies for their care."

"Whatever you need, Excellency," Strauss said. This human was exhausted. "We've arranged for you to stay here as long as you want. Dr. Bloom will help."

"Thank you. The newborn will not be capable of travel for several days. At that time we will transfer them to our ship for the return to Ashentar."

Strauss's bloodshot eyes opened in surprise. "Ashentar? Excuse me, Excellency, but does this mean?—"

"Our mission is over, yes. We have found a worthy recipient for the Knowledge. It was Harrek's wish, of course, but a rashch-claim is not to be ignored." This wasn't precisely true, but the Earth man didn't need to know that. It was convenient for Boroz to allow the claim: it would satisfy the People at home, permitting Boroz to return as a hero, her mission complete, to her second rashch.

"Do you want me to inform my government? Or any government?" This was the first time Boroz saw uncertainty in the Earth man Strauss. She found it amusing.

"Not yet," she said. "We must delay an official announcement until I go through the formality of consulting my sisters. At that point, of course, Mr. Bannekker and your Governor Ruthven and the others should be notified—as should the recipient. Don't worry, Captain. We have not given the Genesis File to your enemies." Nor have we given it to you, she thought with some satisfaction. "Here now!"

One of the newborn had made a reflexive movement with a greater arm, causing Dr. Bloom to back off. Boroz slipped past him and picked up the new brother, moving it to a second bed across the room. "What do you want me to do?" the doctor asked.

"Keep them apart, when they are both awake, which will be soon. Don't be timid with them, either. They're strong and I doubt that you can hurt them." To Strauss she said, "Let us go."

The doctor said, "Uh, tell me, Ambassador, before you go. Which one is Harrek?"

Boroz paused. "The memories of the rashch-brother go to both newborn, yet one will submerge them beneath a new personality, while the other will regain itself. It is impossible to predict . . . sometimes we do not know for months or years. But think of this: both newborn will bite you. One is likely to do it when you aren't looking. *That* will be Harrek."

An hour later Strauss sneaked into the hospital cafeteria looking for something to eat. What he found was Jeremy Clayton asleep on a chair, his head resting on the table in front of him, the remains of a vended meal pushed to one side.

Strauss hated to wake him, knowing that he'd been through an interrogation. Strauss hadn't taken part, but he'd observed. If nothing else, it kept Lippert from playing bad cop with the kid. Jeremy struck Strauss as being honest, fairly bright, and a bit on the quiet side, though you could probably blame that on fatigue.

Why was he hanging around here?

Strauss got himself a cup of coffee and a doughnut. The West Union hospital was barely more than a clinic, and the cook, if there was one, was probably taking care of patients. Or dealing with some of Boroz's requests.

He took a seat across from the kid and vowed that they would have to force him to rise again. Eventually you had to give in to fatigue and depression, and now was the time. Strauss hadn't felt this worn out and useless since Brownsville. In the space of five days he'd lied and been lied to again and again by superiors, subordinates, and anyone who came within range. He'd seen the most basic tasks screwed up, he'd been shot at, he'd given his share of bad instructions . . . he should probably offer his resignation the moment he got back to Austin. He had his twenty years. He'd never be missed.

The funny thing was, no one was going to ask for his resignation or accept it. As far as Texas was concerned, Strauss had made a good save from a very bad situation. Lisa Marquez and Harrek were back where they belonged, and the Genesis File had been kept out of the hands of the Californians *and* the Africans. An outlaw had been killed, but that was a CSA problem: everyone else had come through relatively unscathed. The cost was just a few million Texas dollars.

As government operations went, it was a hell of a bargain.

Best of all, Strauss thought, from this point on all the decisions would be made by persons with fancier titles and greater responsibilities. Strauss was going to a football game.

Jeremy was awake now, rubbing his eyes and running his hands through his hair. "Hi."

"Good morning. You're Jeremy Clayton." The boy nodded. "Tim Strauss, Texas Rangers. I'm sorry to say that I was in charge of that operation yesterday."

"I thought I'd seen you before. On Willow Ridge?"

"Yes. I was probably on my back. That guy Prescott was a pretty good shot. One bolt damn near blew my truck apart. I was lucky."

"I guess he was too scared to think. I know I was."

"Well, it was an unfortunate situation for just about everybody. Except Ben Clayton—your father, I believe."

"Yeah? What about him?"

"He was hit by a piece of shrapnel—nothing too serious. But when they ran a complete medical scan to check for fragments they found an advanced case of lung cancer. They're going to start treating him for it today. He should be able to go home in a few weeks. Within a year, if he keeps up the treatments, he'll be good as new."

"I didn't know."

"I didn't think so." It was seeing the elder Clayton's physical condition that, more than anything, convinced Strauss of Arrowsmith's isolation. Nobody died of lung cancer any more, not even in the CSA. "He was treated and released while you were with the soldiers."

Jeremy frowned. "Isn't treatment like that expensive? Money's not something we have."

"Well, that's one thing you and I need to discuss," Strauss said. "You have more resources than you know. Have you ever heard of the Genesis material?"

"Yeah. The Hocq have it and everybody wants it."

"You've got it."

Jeremy was silent for a moment. "I don't understand."

"The Hocq have licensed the Genesis File to you, Jeremy Clayton. There's nothing to sign, nothing you need to do. I don't think you can even *refuse* at this point. But they have designated you as their sole agent on Earth. Whatever is contained in that File belongs to you, to sell or license or give away as you see fit."

"Why me?"

"Ask Harrek and Boroz. The Hocq said from the very beginning that they planned to license the Genesis material to a 'worthy party' on Earth. We assumed they meant a government. So much for assumptions."

"I don't feel 'worthy.' "

"Maybe you're not. But to the Hocq you are. I couldn't get Boroz to tell me—I don't know that I'd understand her if she did—but they saw in you a responsible person. Someone who was willing to do things for other people that they couldn't do themselves, even if it meant getting hurt. I think that's how *they* define intelligence . . . it has nothing to do with systems of government or whether you misuse atomic power or anything like that."

"I've never been to school. How am I going to understand what's in the File?"

"The Hocq obviously don't see that as a problem. Maybe that's in your favor. You have innocence and curiosity on your side. It may take you years to know what to do with the File. Take my advice:

don't worry about it. The human race has waited thousands of years for something like this . . . a few more years won't hurt."

Strauss felt as if he'd fallen into a TV quiz show. *You've just won a billion dollars in cash! Will you keep it, or will you trade it for whatever's behind door number three?* He half expected Jeremy to jump up and down, shouting for joy . . . but Jeremy didn't. As much as anyone could, he seemed to grasp the importance of what had happened to him, and to accept it.

Maybe that was why the Hocq chose him.

Jeremy started to laugh. "It just occurred to me that I'm going to be getting lots of advice from people from now on."

"For the rest of your life, I expect."

"Well, anyone who wants to talk to me will have to come here."

"Really? You could go anywhere on Earth now, see anyone you want to see. Arrowsmith isn't much of a life."

"No, it isn't, not now. But, you see, Captain, that's the problem in out-of-the-way places like this. The young people leave rather than try to make life better. Up until ten minutes ago *I* was going to leave, too. Kelleher's was going to give me a job. I was ready to move to town. But the Genesis File changes things. I grew up saying I believed in principles and not establishments and never knew what that meant. But I'm beginning to get the idea. I still like Arrowsmith's principles. And for the time being, that's where I belong."

Strauss looked at his watch. "God, it's after seven. Boroz wanted to see you at seven. I think she's going to hand over the File."

"How?"

"I don't have any idea. All I know is that I'm supposed to deliver you to her."

Jeremy stood up. "Okay. But after we're done there, would it be all right if I visited Harrek?"

Strauss smiled. "I think that can be arranged."

EPILOGUE

Arrowsmith, Spring

"Let me have her for a while," Jeremy said.

Heather looked up from the feeding and frowned. "Jeremy Clayton, it's still the middle of the night! You can't take a baby *outside*—"

"I just want to hold her. Besides, she's tough, and it's nice out. And I'll be gone soon."

"Well . . . hurry back."

"Five minutes." He kissed Heather and took the warm bundle in his arms as he headed out the back door of Hill House.

It was still so early on a spring morning that the eastern sky held just a hint of rose and gold. Overhead the stars blazed brightly.

The baby burped. "Feel better now, Lisa?" He received a cooing sound in reply.

Lisa Marquez had been true to her word. Shortly after the new year she and her friend Teri Pedroza had come to visit. Of course, it was a short visit—Lisa was on parole from a Texan minimum security prison—but she seemed happy.

She claimed to have no regrets.

She brought news of the Hocq departure from Earth. Jeremy tried to follow the news, but he'd been so *busy*—

"Here you go, honey." Wide awake, she looked up at him with her green eyes. Carefully, he held her up so that she could see the sky. She waved one of her tiny hands.

"Oh, you want that, do you? It's too big for a little girl. But just wait a few years." He hugged her close again.

There was new light in the kitchen. That would be Ben, up and about, on his way to milk the cows. He and Dan Aucheron were in the middle of a month-old argument about the new herd. Dan maintained that you could train them to give milk at a decent hour . . .

Jeremy had to be on the move himself. Heather would be missing Lisa, Elizabeth would be wanting to say good-bye, and Red Hoerner was probably on his third cup of coffee down at the Sweet Pea, waiting to give him a ride to Dubuque. It would be a long trip this time—two weeks—but he had learned that he couldn't teach himself everything he wanted to know. He had to spend some time with instructors.

He passed beneath the wind machine on the way back to the house, touching it for luck. High overhead the new rotor turned gently in the morning breeze, looking down on the open road that stretched to town, to Texas, and beyond.